戲劇館

戲 劇 館

複製新娘
THE BRIDE AND HER DOUBLE

作者──汪其楣
主編──吳興文
責任編輯──陳懿文・沈斐文

發行人──王榮文
出版發行──遠流出版事業股份有限公司
臺北市汀州路 3 段 184 號 7 樓之 5
郵撥／0189456-1
電話／2365-1212　傳真／2365-7979
香港發行──遠流(香港)出版公司
香港北角英皇道 310 號雲華大廈 4 樓 505 室
電話／2508-9048　傳真／2503-3258
香港售價／港幣 100 元

法律顧問──王秀哲律師・董安丹律師
著作權顧問──蕭雄淋律師

2000 年 3 月 16 日　初版一刷
行政院新聞局局版臺業字第 1295 號
售價新台幣 300 元(缺頁或破損的書,請寄回更換)
版權所有・翻印必究 Printed in Taiwan
ISBN957-32-3909-4

遠流博識網
http://www.ylib.com.tw E-mail:ylib@yuanliou.ylib.com.tw

汪其楣 — 著

複製新娘

THE BRIDE AND HER DOUBLE

By Chi-Mei Wang

English Translation by Chi-Mei Wang
and Jeannie M. Woods

出 版 緣 起

定場詩——為戲劇館揭幕

戲劇閱讀的時代來臨了。

人類的想像力透過文字，成為呼風喚雨的語言，成為激盪心靈的場景，成為情緒綿延、思質起伏、不易言喻的，感性上的認知。

觀劇的即時性、臨場感，相對於私密閱讀的無遠弗屆、不限時空。與眾同歡共泣的集體行為，相對於在一己的當下，就形成最小單位之劇場的恣意與精準，不僅在今日的都市生活中互補並存，而且造成分享熱鬧與探索門道之間更為雋永的循環。

戲劇既是一個高度發展的現代社會中最成熟的表達方式，戲劇亦被視為學習行為中最自然有效的摹擬、感染與散播。台灣戲劇活動頻繁，成為不可忽視的文化動力，各年齡、各階層對舞台演出有無盡的興趣與嚮往，許多人透過劇場這樣的藝術與紀律，凝聚了集體的心靈，展現了個體獨特的才華，迸發了性情深層的創造力，在舊有制度和觀念的重重障礙下，台灣劇場的創作，仍然有令人亮眼心動的表現。這樣的創作人才和創作影響值得鼓勵和累積，而未來人文藝術永續發展中對於戲劇資源與教材的渴求，更使遠流責無旁貸地負起開設戲劇館的使命。

目前以出版台灣各劇種的創作為主，外來作品為輔。戲劇文學，演出圖譜、記實，劇場各項設計及聲光圖、文錄，表、導演思維與實踐的闡述探討，劇場相關藝術與製作的原理、方法及科技種種，都是館裡的戲碼。

戲劇觀眾及讀者將在劇場及網路內外滋生、互動，戲劇藝術家和劇場工作者，在戲劇館內外也有更大的空間和不同的表達機會，透過不斷的搬演與閱讀，甚至殊途另類的再製作、再發揮，屬於大眾的戲劇館，提供藝術經驗多元的流通與薪傳的未來。

戲劇開館，精采可期。作為出版者，在此為您提綱挈領、暗示劇情，一如傳統戲曲的演員粉墨登場之時，先吟唱一曲定場詩詞，與觀眾一同期待所推出連臺好戲的無限興味。

王榮文

複製新娘

THE BRIDE AND HER DOUBLE

By Chi-Mei Wang

English Translation by Chi-Mei Wang
and Jeannie M. Woods

目次

說明與感謝

　　志民跟我講好了，要再在一起作一齣戲，於是有了一九九八年夏天開排，秋熟上演的《複製新娘》。製作人他，本來想的是另一個劇本，後來出了問題，我就義無反顧的自己動手寫。志民常常熱情地替我打氣，也一本正經的批評我，就像他小時候；十幾年前，他曾是我的主修學生、導演助理、音樂助理和男主角；但現在已身為最熱門的劇團果陀的團長，於是他和妻子奇樓，一起沉著且溫柔的監視我，我這個編導也就每天每晚勤奮地修戲。而為了讓我天天都能用主排練室，他們還另外租了一個場地，方便團中其他的劇目也能同時進行演練。呵呵——那真是一個長長的夏季。

　　《複製新娘》寫台灣每年七億市場的賺錢的行業——婚紗攝影；也寫世代做新娘的女子，婚前、婚後，喜悅與悲哀，以及她們從身不由己的世界裡，如何敏感到真實的自己，冀求自主的自己。

　　一如太婆秀貞，沒有「自己的房間」，只有一只針線籃，在女紅繡羅間找尋方塊字，成為她僅有的精神世界，青梅竹馬的情郎也是她唯一的外界通路，沒有愛情的婚姻，使她沒有了自我，失去了美麗與生命。她也是過去數百年來漢文化中的女子表徵。

　　二如外婆君美，有機會讀書，也許也能自選對象，然而為家計兒女辛勞一生，年老時不放棄自我追求，活得更為勇健光采。就是我們現在常常見到各階層的阿媽，不僅活動力強，而且常流露對知性的追求、珍惜，補償婚姻消磨的志趣、理想。

而錦華是我北一女初、高中同學的典型，是社會與人生跑道上的健將，多為理工、生化博士，不放棄事業，不放棄和丈夫終身戀愛，是因為校歌中有「齊家治國，一肩雙挑」的句子？這兩年大家在各自的跑道中稍有喘息，方能相聚，三十幾年歷經裡外各項重任的她們，在我眼中仍是十幾歲的真淳。她們常是完美的母親，亦常有驚人的兒女；而人生已無所堪驚，甜蜜一下、浪漫片刻又何妨，所以讓錦華來到劇中。

驚人的女兒裴裴和繽繽，其實是真實人生裡兩個世代的乖女孩。她們的心事在舞台上略略鋪張出來，她們其實活在一個甚受制約的思想染缸裡，我只是在意年輕女孩本身所感受的壓力、責任和她們所期盼、尋找的包容與開闊。

我參考年輕女孩子們口中的故事，她們自己的，母親、阿姨的，阿祖、阿太的；楊翠所著《日據時代婦女解放運動之研究》、江文瑜主編的《消失中的台灣阿媽》、《阿媽的故事》和《阿母的故事》，更提供了現在年輕演員感知長輩角色鮮活的語言和意態。詩人席慕蓉膾炙人口的許多名句，我移用在最年輕的角色──三位國中生身上，他們自然成誦，朗朗上口，還入樂成歌。就像很多遍佈世界慕蓉的年輕讀者那樣。

然而最重要的是婚紗店舌燦生花的 supersales，我與助理走訪婚紗展和中山北路、愛國東路的鋪子。演員們也入虎穴實地觀察、鑽探。得虎子的不少，被虎吻的更多，居然做田野的被迷得暈陶陶，立即簽單！婚紗店的 sales 本事之大，超過常人的想像。

編劇、演出的趣事說不完；在台中、台南、高雄巡迴時，我們也入境媚俗，把中山北路改成三民路、民生路和中山路，果真台灣每一個城市都有婚紗街。也把傳統市場如水仙宮、成功市場、建國市場這樣的名號，以及公園、社區文康中心都照樣改了，也引起當地觀眾會心的共鳴，說到當地的結婚、離婚率，還往往引起觀眾純情的尖叫。

語言是這個跨越世代又承載推銷術的劇本中重要的元素。但是美籍導演 Jeannie Woods 卻在抵台做交換教授的第二週，完全聽不懂中文的狀況下，憑著節目單上英文劇情摘要，而能充分領會內容和角色精要。她喜歡我導戲的舞台手法，她讚賞這個主題。於是她和我約定，要在半年內把《複製新娘》譯成英文。我和她成了走廊上定期大聲講英文、快筆寫英文的兩個奇怪的身影。翻譯之初有點慢，有點難，我必須解釋很多。譯到三分之一，就覺得容易一些，而且 Dr.Woods 很開心，一方面她覺得能更認識台灣歷史和社會的變遷，另一方面常被形形色色的角色的語言逗得更為興奮和感動。她會說：英文裡好像沒有這個，我回去再謅。下次見面，換做我對她寫回來的妙句拍案叫絕。

英譯的 The Bride and Her Double 竟然就在無痛苦狀態下完成了。此時我伏案整理劇本，與靜婷反覆推敲之際，仍會想起去年夏天，怎麼就這樣在一群好朋友設計家們的擁簇下，在一堆年輕演員的熱汗中，就做出來了這樣一齣戲。製作人夫婦都滿意，奇樓還會為她看過十幾遍的劇情落淚。據說賣座在去年比較「低迷」的情況下，還不錯。我心中稍鬆，生怕老師給學生主持的劇團導戲賠了本，就說不過去了。出版劇本，在台灣其實也還一直是賠本的志業，在一個看戲熱情洋溢，而未必嗜讀劇本的社會裡，還好有遠流董事長王榮文這種人，堅挺著永續文化事業的寬厚肩膀，讓透過對白和舞台提示的字裡行間，馳騁想像力的豐富過程，也成為廣大讀者心靈活動的一部分，也促使我們戲劇創作的點點滴滴逐漸匯入文化的長河。

首演資料

果陀劇場製作

1998 年 9 月 11 日首演於台北新舞台

製作人　梁志民

編劇、導演　汪其楣

舞台設計　林克華

燈光設計　張贊桃

服裝設計　蔡毓芬

舞蹈設計　何曉玫

音樂設計　王柏森

舞台監督　紀宗儀

編導及排演助理　楊靜婷、王立民

暖身領導　傅仰曄

演員

顏芳馨、蔡櫻茹、藍玉萍、秦安蒂、傅仰曄、邱書峰、張碧珊、
黃毓霖、蘇雅貞、王祥至、余威震、王永慶、李奇勳、李武錚、
葉婉如、張莉卿、鍾欣志、洪鵬鎮、邱楷婷、陳祥純、黃浩洸、
陳世文、洪久婷、姜富琴、謝宜靜

場景

　　本劇的主要場景在一家位於台北市中山北路的婚紗店。店的內外以平台區隔。

　　接近舞台正中央是接待處，擺飾著明式的古董桌椅和獨特的鮮花造型。舞台右區，地板有深淺相間的菱形圖案，及一道向外延伸、底座設有燈泡的走道。這個區域也是 sales 與客人談話，或經裝置後進行攝影的地方，牆上懸吊著婚紗禮服。稍後方還有一座可以折疊或開展的弧形鏡子屏風。

　　牆片之間有通道，後牆有大片大片的落地窗口，可以望到後街的招牌或景物。接待處右後有一座輕巧的樓梯可以通往二樓的一間造型試裝室，那裡也放著一整排色彩鮮豔的婚紗禮服，樓上後窗望出去有藍天白雲的景片。

　　舞台左邊可通往街道附近的小方場。靠近舞台的左側有路燈、花圃、樹木。左後方有一個通往巷道的開口。

　　全劇不換景，僅以道具的上下及燈光的變化表達不同的時空。

　　有些區域也可用做戶外的咖啡座、外婆君美的房間、錦華家居的小餐桌，和繽繽與朋友碰面的地方等等。

人物介紹

主要角色

裴　裴　：約 25 歲，正在拍婚紗。與 Tony ，也與小周。

Tony　：裴裴的男友。

小　周　：裴裴的男友。

母親錦華　：裴裴與繽繽的母親，約 50 出頭。生化博士，內外雙挑的賢妻良母。

丈　夫　：裴裴與繽繽的父親。

外婆君美　：錦華的母親，約 80 歲。

太婆秀貞　：君美的母親，約 100 歲，已身故。

情　郎　：太婆秀貞青梅竹馬的玩伴。

繽　繽　：裴裴的妹妹，約 14 歲，國中生。

世　文　：繽繽的男友。

瑞　琪　：繽繽的女友。

二十一世紀台北尖端婚紗攝影禮服的員工群

經理 Jeff 兼攝影

造型師 Andy

攝影師

攝影助理阿浩

sales 婉

sales 勳

sales 祥

sales 武

sales 婷

sales 莉

sales 鵬

次要角色 （可由婚紗店的員工群，甚至主要角色扮飾）

序幕

新娘（可由 sales 莉改扮）

新郎（攝影師）

男方的親戚

上半場 第五景

秀貞父（造型師 Andy）

秀貞夫（經理 Jeff）

喜婆（sales 祥）

僕婦一

僕婦二

僕婦三

小妾（可由 sales 婷改扮）

上半場　第七景

A 桌女客男客

B 桌女客男客

C 桌女客男客

D 桌女客男客

上半場　第八景

姨婆阿梅

校長（造型師 Andy）

阿公（sales 勳）

下半場　第一景

阿婆甲（sales 婷）

阿婆乙（sales 祥）

阿公甲（sales 武）

阿公乙（阿浩）

阿公丙（sales 鵬）

教練（可由太婆秀貞改扮）

複製新娘劇本

上半
場

上半場

楔子

（在音樂聲中幕起，舞台上一幅凝止的傳統送嫁景象。新娘穿著雪白的無肩低胸禮服，大蓬裙，裙尾曳地，一公尺餘。新郎一襲白色金扣小禮服，捧著一束玫瑰，親友穿紅戴綠，某位嬸婆正展示著手中的紅包。婚紗店的攝影師、造型師、助理和 sales，身戴紅色名條及配花全員出動，打理新人周遭的一切。也有一位手執有頭有尾的竹枝，上面垂著一塊五花肉；另一位則雙手高舉一個又大又圓的竹篩，保護新人。在巴洛克風格的「草螟仔弄雞公」的音樂聲中，以舞蹈化的姿態進行手邊的工作，婚紗店的經理帶領大家開始這一場婚紗店主辦的「送嫁」。）

經理 Jeff　　準備好了嗎？（環顧四周）我們可以開始了。可以
　　　　　　了嗎？（要眾人一一 Check）

造型師 Andy　新娘？唉喲，新娘子不要哭，新娘子不要哭，妝都
　　　　　　糊了。（安慰新娘，幫她止淚補妝。）

Sales 婉　　（站在新郎、新娘中間正後方）前面新郎不要太緊張。
　　　　　　來，你去幫他擦擦汗。
　　　　　　──好，準備。
　　　　　　時辰到了！
　　　　　　送新娘子出閣了！

經理 Jeff　　（以鏗鏘的台語突顯著賀詞的韻味）

今天是好日子，兩家結連理。

——來這裡拍一張。

竹篩——拍一張。

新娘靜靜站在這，

不要像是電火條，

新郎你的 pose 也免操煩，

送出手頭的 rose 眞大板。

（新郎依言把手中的捧花交給新娘，但擺出傻里傻氣的單腿下跪鏡頭，眾人大樂鼓掌，造型師 Andy 順勢對新郎的家人以台語唱作俱佳的祝福）

造型師 Andy　　一對佳人結尪某，

二人牽手共甘苦，

三世修來眞福報，

四季平安好前途。

（嬸婆開心的給他一個紅包）

Sales 勳　　來，丟扇子，新娘子，——拍一張。

（新娘丟扇子的動作悲喜交加，欲丟還留，在身邊繞了半天，才丟出去。眾人的目光和身體在音樂節奏中隨著她丟扇子的動作誇張的起伏。）

造型師 Andy　　覆水難收，真情永久，覆水難收，真情永久。（手
　　　　　　　　中拿著一碗水，也往前方潑出去。）

Sales 勳　　　好，現在從這邊去，禮車在那邊巷口，等一下上高
　　　　　　　速公路比較不會塞車。
　　　　　　　來，小心她的裙子，好。

（新郎、新娘開始往前走，大家在身邊打點、呵護著，也有兩人特別蹲
著走，整理新娘的裙擺。送嫁的行列沿舞台前緣大轉彎，往舞台左後方
的門口走出去，沿途聽見經理鏗鏘有致的祝賀詞）

經理 Jeff　　　嘴對嘴，萬年富貴；
　　　　　　　手牽手，天長地久。
　　　　　　　新郎真古錐，新娘有夠水；
　　　　　　　今日結尪某，明年生鐵鎚。
　　　　　　　恭喜恭喜真恭喜，新郎學問了不起，
　　　　　　　新娘賢慧知鄉里，二人適配無底比。

（行列從舞台左往右走出去，觀眾可以透過門窗，見到他們熱鬧的身
影，婚紗店的員工也在後面興奮的相送。當親屬的身影即將隱沒時，突
然聽到造型師 Andy 大叫）

造型師 Andy	不要回頭！（眾 sales 跟著喊）
眾 Sales	不要回頭，不要回頭！

（大夥目送新人上車後，才全身放鬆，重新從左邊的門，走進舞台，邊說邊拿下身上的名條、花朵，邊收拾婚紗店內外的東西。）

經理 Jeff	咻，終於把他們送上車了。
Sales 婉	沒想到這個 case 花招這麼多。新娘子站多久，我就陪她站多久。站得差點「替腿」。
Sales 祥	以後接這種從店裡出嫁的不能打太多折扣，時間拖太長了。
造型師 Andy	又要算時辰，又要一大早起來化妝，還要陪新郎家的三嬸婆聊天。
經理 Jeff	不過娘家不在台北的，把婚紗店當娘家從這裡出嫁，是我們招牌節目之一，花招是我們想的，就別抱怨了。
Sales 婉	（怪笑）阿浩，你好扯。那塊豬肉還買錯，笑死人。
阿浩	我怎麼知道那個肉攤老闆會趁我不注意把肉剁成一塊一塊的，然後又趁我不注意包起來。
造型師 Andy	誰叫你去晴光市場買，還好我趁早打開來檢查。
阿浩	傳統市場的豬肉還是比較好吃的啦！
Sales 婉	神經病，那塊豬肉又不是來燉紅燒肉的。

Sales 祥	你打開來看幹嘛，想吃生豬肉啊？
造型師 Andy	還好我檢查，才來得及趕快去買一塊。（改變話題）下午客人又馬上要來了，今天有幾個？
Sales 婉	（湊過去，小聲問他）她給你包多少？
造型師 Andy	（拿出紅包，從封口目測，微笑）還可以啦！
阿浩	六點有一個，裴裴小姐。拍訂婚綠野香波系列，已經在化妝了。
Sales 婷	八點有一個，好像也叫什麼裴？不會是同一個人吧？他們要拍比較華貴的、古典的。
經理 Jeff	等一下就知道了。
	小婉，你看你，你一聊天精神真好，忘了腿痠。你進去看一下那個頭頂上的花飾，還有帽子什麼的先拿上來。
	阿浩！燈具。

第一景

（浪漫音樂聲中 Tony 牽著裴裴從更衣間走出來。）

Sales 婷　　　裴裴小姐，都準備好了，請過來這邊。

裴裴　　　　（兩人看著落地窗的長鏡，並肩顧盼生姿）你覺得我戴
　　　　　　這個花怎麼樣？

Tony　　　　還不錯，可以上台演戲了。（嘻笑一番，sales 把高
　　　　　　矮不同的柱子、布幔、花飾等道具安排好了。）

經理 Jeff　　來，我們先拍一組希臘神廟，站在柱子旁，頭看這
　　　　　　邊。

造型師 Andy　公主要像希臘的小女神，嬌羞可愛。

Sales 婷　　　牙齒露出來。（他們拍了幾張。）

經理 Jeff　　來，再一組羅馬假期。（眾助理迅速改換現場布置，
　　　　　　移去大柱子，搬上小噴泉。）

造型師 Andy　很好，公主，很漂亮，來，笑，像奧黛莉赫本，公
　　　　　　主，雙手伸出來。王子，來，把腿翹起來，你就像
　　　　　　那個電影裡的記者吧。

經理 Jeff　　王子的眼睛再炯炯有神一點，我要拍了。（按快門）
　　　　　　很好！

Tony	等一下，我還有道具（從 sales 手中接過預備好的花束）……木玫瑰。
裴裴	你怎麼還記得！
Tony	當然記得！
裴裴	我種在陽台上那棵現在還只有綠葉子。
Tony	放心，到了秋天，葉子都掉光，整片牆就開滿了這些花。 來，我們拍一張妳拿花的。
造型師 Andy	呦，特別的花給特別的妳！
經理 Jeff	看鏡頭，保持微笑，自然一點。就這樣，不要動（按）。來，再一張。（按）

（裴裴將花故意伸到 Tony 的鼻子前，眾人笑。）

經理 Jeff	這樣拍也不錯。

（Sales 移動道具，造型師幫兩人整理衣裝、頭髮，兩人自顧自的說話）

Tony	好想去義大利一年。
裴裴	你不是說要跟我去巴黎嗎？
Tony	今年太多人去法國了吧！ How about Italy ？ 我們可以先旅行半年，剩下半年什麼都不做，好好

畫畫。

裴裴　　　　聽起來蠻好的，而且那家 furniture design 公司一直
　　　　　　要我去做他們的 decorator ，如果跟你去義大利的
　　　　　　話，我就可以多學一點。

　　　　　　（在下列的台詞中，興奮的做出舞姿）

　　　　　　Florence ！ Venice ！ Rome ！來，試試看這個動作
　　　　　　怎麼樣？

　　　　　　（她大力的旋轉，卻被裙子絆倒）

眾 Sales　　　小心！小心！（Tony 正扶著裴裴要站起來）

造型師 Andy　不要動，這個 pose 很好，王子，腳抬高一點。

經理 Jeff　　　很好！笑！（按）

（他們正準備站起來。）

造型師 Andy　不要動！這個 pose 很好。

　　　　　　就這個樣子。

經理 Jeff　　　再一張！笑！（按）

（剛站好正在拉裙子。）

造型師 Andy　這個好，不要動。

　　　　　　Oh! My God ，像瑪麗蓮夢露，上半身這樣。手抓著

裙子。很好。

經理 Jeff　　　不要動！笑！（按）O.K.。

（轉身吩咐助理，助理們把襯景換成銀藍相間的背幕，也可利用懸吊系統。）

經理 Jeff　　　換下一景，流星系列。（婚紗人員換「流星系列」景。）

Tony　　　　　我參加一個公共藝術的徵件，我一看那評審委員的名單，就知道一定是要弄個沒有人懂的東西，沒有人看得懂的東西，我最會了。

裴裴　　　　　沒有人聽得懂的笑話，你也最會了。

Tony　　　　　妳聽得懂就好了。

經理 Jeff　　　我們來拍這個流星系列！

造型師 Andy
Sales 婷　　　像我們這樣。

（造型師 Andy 、 sales 婷做相擁仰望的示範。）

經理 Jeff　　　假設那裡有一顆流星，許願，看著遠方的星星。有一顆星星掉下來，世界和平。（他們抬頭面帶微笑，繼續聊自己的天）

Tony	我想先去現場看看四周的建築，要不要一起去？去台中。
裴裴	什麼時候？
Tony	不要週末，太擠了，妳蹺班，我們去看了之後還可以到埔里去住一夜。
經理 Jeff	（按）來，換下一個 pose。
造型師 Andy	這個 pose 非常好，腳抬高一點。
裴裴	蹺班度假？好浪漫！就像現在，蹺班，你最會。
經理 Jeff	卡喳。
造型師 Andy	（回頭對經理使眼色）我想差不多了吧？裴裴小姐，妳還滿意嗎？
	（裴裴點頭）
Tony	還不錯，可以了。

（造型師向大家示意可以收東西了，兩人邊取下身上的飾物，脫掉外套，邊往裡面走。）

Tony	等一下妳要不要去 @Live ？
裴裴	今天？不好（她俏皮的眨眨眼睛），我媽要我早點回去。
Tony	妳媽就是這樣。
裴裴	對呀。她每天下班趕回來做晚飯，還要送我妹去上

鋼琴，補習什麼的，然後再回來等我爸吃飯。

Tony　　　　好吧，那我先回去。那明天去？

裴裴　　　　好呀！明天是 Ladies Night ，女生免費入場。

（兩人邊走邊笑沒入舞台右上方。）

（小段音樂。）

第二景

（在上段戲中，裴裴提到母親時，舞台左下方即開始漸亮。這是裴裴家中的一角，她的媽媽錦華，擺設好餐桌的檯布和水果，坐在高背歐風藤椅上，嫻雅地等待。她的丈夫進來，換上拖鞋。）

錦華　　　你回來了。

丈夫　　　我回來了。

錦華　　　猜今天晚飯吃什麼？

丈夫　　　吃什麼？

錦華　　　銀魚莧菜羹。

丈夫　　　嗯……銀魚。

錦華　　　彩虹苦瓜。

丈夫　　　喔……苦瓜。

錦華　　　雞絲拉皮。

丈夫　　　（故意）誰去拉皮？

錦華　　　（過去拍了他一下）是……雞──絲──拉──皮──啦。

錦華　　　你這麼熱，要不要先洗個澡？還是餓了，想先吃飯？哇！今天這麼晚，都快八點了……

（錦華繼續主導以下工作、生活、置物等話題，容光煥發，喜孜孜。丈夫常微笑、點頭，或以手勢反應。）

錦華　　　小狗……？

丈夫　　　早上花豹和阿 B 都出去過了。阿 B 大了，花豹還沒有。

錦華　　　那晚上……

丈夫　　　睡覺前我再帶牠們去散步一次好了。

錦華　　　我們那個會終於開成了，三個 Labs 的協調其實很簡單，只不過是大帳、小帳怎麼匯通的問題，比我們所有的研究案簡單太多了，根本一目了然，真不知道這些男人（輕輕一笑）幹什麼把事情搞得那麼複雜。

丈夫　　　你沒吵架？

錦華　　　我才不會跟人吵架，讓他們去吵。每一邊都講了四、五十分鐘，最後還不是差不多。我心裡真的很想笑，還是必須做出很專注的樣子，在那裡作主席。你呢？你忙不忙？

丈夫　　　今天 Peter 要去武漢，老闆又從香港來 check 那個 CPU 的案子，下午真的很趕。

錦華　　　後面陽台那個木櫃子，下星期會估好價，你說什麼時候開工比較好？

丈夫	你決定好了。
	繽繽快回來了吧？她是去上鋼琴？
錦華	木櫃子的材料大概選的不錯，劉老闆說還是用進口
	比較好。
丈夫	我待會兒出門，可以先去接繽繽回來……裴裴呢？
錦華	你還有事啊！本來我以為你可以跟我一塊去看裴裴
	的……

（兩人談話聲漸小）

（他微笑的點頭，拿起晚報。）

（她過來攔下，多情喜悅的看著他。）

（他努力配合，又不知不覺拿起報紙。）

（她再度迎上來……）

（此區燈光慢慢暗去，婚紗店的燈漸漸變亮。）

第三景

（婚紗店中，裴裴已換上一套華貴象牙色禮服。她站在一幅金紗的布簾前，宛如金色瀑布一般鋪瀉到地面，婚紗店的助理們也在她頭上、身上忙著打點。這段戲開始時，經理 Jeff 正在聽電話；裴裴的另一男友小周，從左舞台後方上，正把手機收線，往前走。）

經理 Jeff　　　公主，周先生說他馬上到。

Sales 莉　　　裴裴小姐，這個造型也很適合妳，真是濃粧淡抹皆相宜，鄉野宮廷都美麗。

經理 Jeff　　　唷，周先生來了，請進。

小周　　　　　Hi，裴，怎麼讓你等我了。

裴裴　　　　　沒關係，妝才剛化好。

造型師 Andy　哇！王子你這套西裝也很帥。不過，我們還是要麻煩你過來這邊，換這件上衣試試看，看和公主站在一起的……感覺！

經理 Jeff　　　你們知道攝影其實重點不是衣服，禮服每一套都好看，重點真的是那種「感覺」啦！

裴裴　　　　　我美不美？

小周　　　　　這還用問嗎？上次開車經過這裡的時候，我就知

	道，妳穿上這套禮服會有多漂亮。
Sales 祥	好。現在 pose 一下，看這邊。
攝影師	來，笑。（按）
Sales 祥	到王子的臉上補一點妝。
攝影師	來，笑。（按）
Sales 祥	這麼漂亮的公主、王子，你們的婚禮一定也很出色。
阿浩	（一面測光）婚期是什麼時候？我們可以提供現場服務。
裴裴	還早。
小周	快了。（與裴裴幾乎同時）

（大夥面面相覷，停了兩秒，又故意發出笑聲。）

攝影師	來，貼近一點，看這邊，笑。（按）
小周	等一下會有人來看妳。
裴裴	真的嗎？誰？阿張和小玲？（小周搖頭）不會吧，Steve 和他 lover？（小周搖頭）小劉跟他老婆？誰？（繼續微笑搖頭）誰？還會有誰？
小周	妳的母親大人。
裴裴	我媽？我不相信——！
小周	真的。她說她會來。 She'll be so proud of you！

裴裴	她說？她怎麼會知道？你告訴她啦？
	唉喲，完了。（微慍）
小周	（對她溫柔的唱出）"You are so beautiful."
攝影師	這樣很好。來，笑。（按）
裴裴	她來一定會說……
小周	她如果對禮服有意見的話，我們就穿一套她喜歡的好了。
	妳上一次不是說有一件淺粉綠的，妳媽會喜歡嗎？
Sales 祥	有時候，媽媽的意見也是可以吸收啦，畢竟結婚的時候，不是只有你們兩個，還有很多長輩在場。
裴裴	（臉色有點難看）給我媽知道就非結不可了。
	你小心，擅自越級，打小報告，給她知道你就別想跟我結婚。
小周	唉！別說的那麼嚴重！
攝影師	來，笑。（拍最後一張）
	我們換 pose。

（小周扶著裴裴的腰，裴裴向後仰，Andy 等把衣服的飄帶整理出漂亮的線條，極盡其形容之能事，讓她握在手中。此時錦華已站在婚紗店門口，看著他們拍照，小周首先發現。）

小周	伯母，您好。

裴裴	（後仰中的裴裴，也看到了媽媽，也發出叫聲）媽——
錦華	（小小鼓掌，對店員們讚許）裴裴，妳好漂亮。（走進店中，環顧四周）裴裴，妳今天挑了幾套呀？
裴裴	沒有啦，就先試拍這一套而已。
錦華	多試幾套嘛，我看這家的樣子都還不錯，比較特別。小周，你說是不是？
小周	（點點頭）相當 quality oriented, （小聲）and the price is reasonable. （裴裴瞪他一眼）
錦華	來都來了，再試幾套，試給我看。
小周	反正妳今天難得有空，我可以在外面等妳們。
Sales 莉	我們這裡有一套是造型師特別推薦的、全新的，要不要試試看？
錦華	是什麼樣式？
Sales 莉	非常有味道，店長要我們特別準備的，在樓上，妳看了就知道。
裴裴	真的嗎？
Sales 莉	就看妳要不要再體會一下這種典雅、高貴的感覺。
裴裴	也好……
攝影師	請走這邊。

（引裴裴往二樓走，錦華跟著上去， sales 莉邊走邊解釋。）

Sales 莉	我們有很多造型新穎的禮服，都放在樓上，不會掛在櫥窗裡，因為怕人家偷拍、抄襲我們的設計。
錦華	眞的嗎？有這種事呀？怎麼不尊重別人的設計著作權呢？
Sales 莉	對呀！有時候在夜市裡會看到我們設計的禮服，在那裡好便宜的賣，心裡都覺得……唉！好難過喔！

（此時他們都已經到達二樓，裴與 sales 莉到掛滿禮服的那一排衣架後換裝，必要時她也會從衣服堆中怪里怪氣的伸出頭來。）

裴裴	媽，我 call 機響了，拜託幫我拿一下。（錦華把 call 機遞到後面。）
	媽，妳手機借我。
錦華	（故意問）妳要打給誰呀？
裴裴	媽妳不要管嘛！（一直按，打不出去）眞是的，怎麼在這棟大樓裡打不出去。
錦華	妳看，妳不說是誰，我的手機就不理妳。喂，你們不是早分手了嗎？
裴裴	我的老母！我跟誰分手？妳那麼開心幹嘛？
錦華	我怎麼啦？我又沒有笑。
裴裴	告訴妳，我不會跟他分手的。
錦華	裴裴，妳不是準備結婚了嗎？

裴裴	我就知道妳會給我壓力。
錦華	我從來不會給妳壓力，任何事。那……妳拍這些照片又是幹什麼呢？
Sales 莉	拍了這麼漂亮造型的婚紗攝影，婚期大概就不會遠了。
裴裴	妳們不是說婚紗可以試拍，滿意才下訂單嗎？
錦華	妳出來給我看看。哇！裴裴，還是這件好看。現在的質料真好……
Sales 莉	這是進口的提花刺繡，「鐵達尼號」的影響。
錦華	妳選這件的話，可以配我的那條珍珠項練。
裴裴	裙擺這邊還挺好看的，但是配珍珠項練的話，有點老氣，小姐，這件我覺得不太像我耶！
Sales 莉	我看還蠻適合妳的，很高貴，和妳的臉型很合啦，這種袖子，很適合妳的肩部……
裴裴	太古典了，媽，這比較像妳的 style（日本腔發音，轉頭對店員說）我想去試剛剛那件蘋果綠鑲邊的。
Sales 莉	我去準備。
裴裴	媽，妳知道我在想什麼嗎？妳就是歌仔戲裡面的老夫人，嫌貧愛富。
錦華	什麼歌仔戲什麼的，又胡說八道。
裴裴	媽，真的，妳什麼事情都在逼我做選擇。
錦華	我是高高興興的來看妳跟小周拍婚紗照，妳怎麼又

講成這個樣子，我是希望……

裴裴　　妳希望我像妳一樣選一個像樣的丈夫……

錦華　　不是，我只是希望妳……過得幸福，希望妳少吃一點苦。

裴裴　　妳希望我像妳一樣選一個像樣的丈夫，有一份穩定的工作，結婚、生孩子、做家庭主婦，還是像妳一樣……做個超級女強人。「我是不能也，亦不為也。」

錦華　　說什麼呀！我每天種花、燒菜、煮咖啡，給全家關燈、蓋被子，還最喜歡跟女兒一起去 shopping 買漂亮的衣服。什麼女強人，說我是超級「女弱人」還差不多。

裴裴　　（裴把外套脫下，拋給媽媽，逕自準備下樓。）

　　　　嗯，妳真的沒聽懂我想說的話。

　　　　媽，我大概還要跟店裡的設計師談一下，好不好，妳不要跟來，還是請我們親愛的「女弱人」先回家，不用等我了。OK？Mom？

　　　　（下樓）

錦華　　（獨自留在台上）其實我只是希望妳嫁一個愛妳的男人……像我一樣？

　　　　像我一樣很好啊，像我一樣有什麼不好。

第四景

（在上段的話尾中，錦華把裴裴禮服的外套無奈的掛上衣架，隨即翻動那一排禮服，並且取出一件在自己身上比了比。）

（音樂淡出，燈光轉為柔和。）

錦華　　做新娘，跟相愛的人結婚，走過花環拱立的紅地
　　　　毯，悠揚的音樂、眾人的讚美與祝福，共同譜出人
　　　　生美麗的詩篇。
　　　　妳不是從小做花童的時候就這樣想嗎？我，我沒有
　　　　做過花童，我們那個時代還沒有機會，還很少啦。

（錦華順手把禮服搭在扶梯的欄杆上。）

　　　　裴裴小的時候，我什麼都給她，四歲就會去牽紗、
　　　　五歲就做花童，連衣服……
　　　　那時候流行小泡泡裙，都給她做一件新的。我沒有
　　　　的，她都有。我五、六歲的時候，還在穿別人剩下
　　　　的舊衣服，進高中才有第一件連身洋裝，還是阿姨
　　　　做的。
　　　　十六歲裴裴已經請同學在家裡開 birthday party 了。
　　　　裴裴那時候功課又好，也已經長的很漂亮了……

（沉醉在記憶中）

那個喜歡裴裴的陳家的小兒子，胖胖的小西裝頭，那天晚上還哭了一場，因為發現裴裴不喜歡他，喜歡別人。

聽說他好像結婚了，娶了台光公司的女兒，好像還不錯，這都是裴裴說的，裴裴不也是快要出嫁了嗎？怎麼還這樣陰陽怪氣、吞吞吐吐的。

她以前不是這樣的，裴裴小的時候多貼心，so sweet，每天放學回家，坐在廚房門口跟我講學校的事情，我不應她，她還生氣。現在，現在一問多了，她就生氣。……老天，我真搞不懂，我們的女兒在想什麼？

（Sales 婉從後面帶著一名助理上來找衣飾。）

Sales 婉　　抱歉，我來拿一下東西。

錦華　　　喔！不好意思，我在等我女兒。

Sales 婉　　剛在換衣服的裴裴小姐嗎？真好命，媽媽這樣疼她，是獨生女嘍？

錦華　　　還有一個小的妹妹，比她小很多，上國中，等於兩個都是獨生女。

Sales 婉　　差這麼遠，會不會不好帶？

錦華	小的還好，有人幫忙。裴裴真的是我一手餵奶推搖籃，另一隻手寫論文這樣帶大的，想起來都不相信。不過那時候年輕，好像不怕累，也不知道苦，一面念學位，一面打工，還做 full time 媽咪，也真的把她帶大了。生第二個的時候還好，我們已經回台灣了。
Sales 婉	（助理找到一件色調古雅的中國式的新娘衣）啊！這件衣服原來在這裡！
錦華	這種古老新娘的嫁衣也有？
Sales 婉	世代新娘的禮服和配件是我們的 specialty，我們這家的攝影師的曾祖父在滿清時代和日本時代就是照相師，拍過的新娘照片都收在博物館裡，我們樓下也有一張。

（此時樓下屏風的特殊燈光漸亮，依稀見到屏風後有一位古裝的新娘，就像站在相框裡的模樣。）

（二樓燈光圈縮小、轉暗，集中在錦華上半身，直到本段戲的結尾，再漸漸暗去。）

錦華	聽我母親說過，我的阿媽就穿那種古早的新娘衣出嫁的。以前還有一張相片，但是八七水災的時候沖掉了，現在都有點記不清楚她的樣子了。可惜我都

沒見過我的阿媽，（充滿神往）她在我母親還很小
的時候就過世了。

Sales 婉　　她一定長得很漂亮，您和裴裴小姐都這麼出色。

錦華　　　哪裡；不過，（她的手不知不覺的抬起到頰邊）我們
都遺傳我母親，和母親的母親的眼睛。

（空靈、悠遠的音樂聲漸起。）

第五景

(年輕女孩時代的太婆秀貞從屏風後出現。婚紗店內已擺置了雕花的月門和古雅的桌椅，三位婚紗店的 sales，扮演秀貞家的僕婦，幫她梳妝打扮，她們的姿態動作以及手中的大手絹都帶著古典的風味。

秀貞捧著她的針線籃，坐在高椅上，拿出一樣繡件，看了兩眼，又把它放回去，然後拿出籃底的方塊字，一張張四方的硬紅紙，上面寫著正楷毛筆字，秀貞拿一個唸一個。)

秀貞　　　　人、口、手、刀、尺、

　　　　　　大、中、小、天、地（唸錯成「他」，被僕婦一糾正為「地」。）

僕婦一　　　地，天──，地──。

秀貞　　　　一、二、三、四、五、

　　　　　　上、下、心、夫、婦。（「婦」字不確定，僕婦一過來瞧一眼馬上就告訴她，「婦」。）

僕婦一　　　婦是什麼？就是妻子，就是新娘。

僕婦二　　　妳就要做新娘了。

秀貞　　　　我不要！（大家輕笑）

僕婦三　　　妳不要也不行，你阿爸都幫你安排好了。

秀貞　　　　我要唸書、認字，我要……

僕婦三　　　妳認字就認字，唸啊，唸……

秀貞　　　　（快速努力的念，不小心打翻針線籃，方塊字也掉了一
　　　　　　地，她一面撿一面讀，眼睛開始看著窗外，像是在等待
　　　　　　什麼人？）
　　　　　　人口手刀尺、大中小天、他……
　　　　　　一二三四五、上下心夫婦、他……他……他……
　　　　　　（眼看窗外）

（遙遠傳來嘹亮的聲音，小情郎出現。）

（在舞台左後正中門口，他一面大聲的唸字，一面蹦跳前進，遊戲般的
到了台邊。）

情郎　　　　一、二、三、四、五　　一、二、三、四、五
　　　　　　大──中──小──
　　　　　　（秀貞雀躍的往外去，他跨著大步、中步、小步，到了
　　　　　　秀貞的門口，然後對他伸出手說）天！

秀貞　　　　（她也伸出手說）他！

（他把秀貞帶出來，兩人快樂的在「屋外」轉圈，然後和諧的帶著動
作，唱這支他倆從小熟悉的歌謠。）

兩人合諧	（歌曲）一、二、三、四、五、六、七——

兩人合諧　　（歌曲）一、二、三、四、五、六、七——

　　　　　　我的朋友在哪裡？

　　　　　　在那（這）裡，在那（這）裡，我的朋友在這裡。

　　　　　　（兩人面對面配合手的動作）

秀貞　　　　上，

情郎　　　　下，

秀貞　　　　心，

情郎　　　　心，（與秀貞同時）

秀貞　　　　夫，

情郎　　　　婦。

（兩人近似舞蹈的動作中，互相戲弄，親暱而依賴，小情郎把秀貞扛起旋轉，秀貞把粉紅方巾蓋在臉上，落地後，情郎把腰帶一端交給秀貞，輕輕牽著她，一起到舞台左下角；他揭開她的頭蓋，她嫣然一笑，頭上的花飾輕輕落下。

此時，婚紗店的右上角，老父、丈夫、喜婆，擺好架勢，趕路般的策馬到左下角，小情侶被拆散，秀貞被拉回。僕婦把門關上。即是把婚紗店中區接待處的景片打開，延展成一道繪有彩霞的門面。

柔美的音樂轉成緊張的鑼鼓聲，秀貞被父親蓋上巨大的紅蓋頭方巾，被送入丈夫的懷抱。秀貞閃躲著，不願被丈夫強行掀開紅蓋頭，但終至無力，丈夫把紅蓋頭拿在手，在她身上拂動、耍弄。再用紅蓋頭像繩索一般套住她，把她抱到椅子上。鑼鼓聲轉劇，丈夫把紅蓋頭展開，遮住顫抖的新娘，完成他得意的新婚之夜。秀貞從丈夫身上下來後，丈夫把紅蓋頭揉成一團，丟給她，秀貞無言的接在胸前，順從的以方巾的一角給丈夫擦汗。

娶親的嗩吶聲又響起，喜婆又送進一個花枝招展的姑娘，丈夫走過去逗弄小妾，兩人打情罵俏；秀貞此刻已到屏風後快速改裝，一轉身出來已成了有身孕的新婦。小妾向秀貞行禮，秀貞面無表情往旁邊走去，丈夫也走過去對她安撫；此刻小妾也到屏風後面改裝，出來後成了個大肚子的妾。她得意的挺著肚子，見丈夫還在秀貞那邊，立刻忌妒撒潑，用大肚子刻意東頂西撞，撞翻椅子，撞歪了門，丈夫速速跑過來，安撫小妾，小妾佯裝不睬，三番四次後，兩人嬉鬧相擁到後方去，秀貞在一旁看在眼裡，若即若離，全不在意。）

僕婦一	妳怎麼不在乎呢？
僕婦二	被她爬到頭上去就不好玩了。（秀貞嘆氣、搖頭）
僕婦一	到底還是不歡喜，
僕婦二	否則嘆什麼氣？
秀貞	我在想心事。
僕婦一	想什麼心事，
僕婦二	說給我們聽聽。
秀貞	你們不會懂的。
僕婦一	新娘子的心事我們不懂得？
僕婦二	哪還有誰懂得啊！

秀貞　　　　　我只想死，死了什麼都好。

僕婦一　　　　唉！那就奇了，新娘的新衣服還閃亮亮的，鈕釦都
　　　　　　　硬挺挺的，繡花鞋底都沒踩髒，珠花、耳環戴也戴
　　　　　　　不完？（小聲到她身邊警告）
　　　　　　　講什麼死啊死的，觸霉頭，別把全家所有的人都惹
　　　　　　　得不爽快。

秀貞　　　　　死了就爽快，我嫁的不是我中意的郎，我心中不爽快。

（兩位僕婦面面相覷，有點吃驚，但秀貞不理會她們，逕自往外走。她
坐在門口台階上，把籃中的方塊字一面拋向空中，一面聲音嘶啞顫抖的
唸著。）

秀貞　　　　　人　口　手　刀　尺
　　　　　　　大　中　小　天　地

（自從身邊的秀貞被奪走後，小情郎拾了她頭上的珠花，常常站在村中
的某處，眺望遠處的姑娘，別人的新娘。

舞台上可以處理成這樣：在上面秀貞成婚的段落發生過程中，小情郎以
極緩慢的速度，沿著舞台左側外緣移動，然後再站在舞台左後的開口後
方，至此他佇立的身影逐漸向前移動。觀眾也正式注意到他，他走到舞
台正中間時，緩緩開口。）

情郎　　　　那邊的山上沒有樹，

　　　　　　樹上也沒有鳥，

　　　　　　河裡沒有魚，

　　　　　　那邊的河裡連水都沒有了，

　　　　　　那邊的人，

　　　　　　也沒有眼淚了。

　　　　　　她一定在找我。

　　　　　　她——她——（無力的蹲下）

　　　　　　她她她她她她她她（輕緩地唱）

　　　　　　在這裡——在這裡——我的——在這裡

秀貞　　　　（也哀聲唱著）一　二　三　四　五

（兩人的聲音重疊。突然燈光急轉成閃電般的紅光，繞台數匝之際，兩人在想像的世界中相見。）

情郎
秀貞　　　　　上　下　心　夫　婦

（兩人悲喜交加，一個字一個字演化著動作，幾乎重複青梅竹馬時歡樂的遊戲模式。但小情郎殷切卻更沉重，秀貞從羞慚苦楚到悲傷及超脫。）

秀貞　　　　那邊山上有一棵樹。

情郎	這是妳頭上的花。
秀貞	你一直站在樹底下。
情郎	撿起妳的花，我知道再也見不到妳了。
秀貞	要是能再看你一眼。
情郎	要是能見到妳。
秀貞	就不再心傷。（心的動作）
情郎	就不要心傷。要是再在妳身邊，要是再把花給妳戴上。
秀貞	（主動）來，我跟著你唸。那邊山上，有一棵樹。
情郎	不要心傷。（抬頭）
秀貞	你在樹下，我跟著你唸。我們在樹下。
情郎	山上有樹。
秀貞	山上有兔。
情郎	河裡有魚。（魚動作）
秀貞	河裡有驢。（魚動作）
情郎	樹上有鳥。
秀貞	樹上有「鳥仔」，樹下有腳。
情郎	樹下不會有腳。
秀貞	那樹下有什麼？
情郎	樹下有人。
秀貞	有人。
情郎	樹下有人，人，在等人。人，在等妳。
秀貞	他，在等妳。

情郎	樹下有腳，他，在等妳，河裡有魚。
秀貞	人，在等你。
兩人	等妳（你），等妳（你）。

（悠揚柔美的音樂聲中，兩人翩然起舞，情深醉人。舞終，秀貞再被輕輕放回門前，她蹲坐在地，面對門內，她的手向後伸，手指緊緊勾著他的，終於被放開，小情郎蹤影消散，秀貞黯然踱回屏風後。）

（二樓燈光漸亮。）

Sales 鵬	（拿果汁上樓）您的果汁，請用。
錦華	謝謝。
	阮阿媽跟阮阿母講，要嫁，就要嫁自己恰意的人，我阿母也跟我講按呢。我對裴裴也是一樣啊！裴裴就是不聽我的話，把我的話都聽反，繽繽就不會。
Sales 鵬	繽繽？是裴裴小姐的妹妹嗎？
錦華	繽繽是我的小女兒。我該打個電話了。
Sales 鵬	這個交給我好了。（接回杯子。）
錦華	（拿出手機，真的不通。）奇怪，我的手機怎麼真的打不出去。
Sales 鵬	那到樓下打好了，沒問題的。

（二人準備下樓，燈漸暗。）

第六景

（輕快的音樂響起，夾雜著各種 call 機聲，繽繽從舞台左下方，快步走進她的光區。）

繽繽　　　（call 機聲）530——我想妳。

　　　　　嗯，妳功課作完，在想我啊？好，我也來 call 妳。

　　　　　5130。

瑞琪　　　（瑞琪從舞台的右下方興奮的奔跑上）5130——我也想妳。

繽繽　　　（call 機又響了）1177155 u 這是什麼呀？我來解一解，1 是 I，177 是 M，155 是 ISS，MISS 對了……

瑞琪　　　（繼續按）7799

繽繽　　　I MISS YOU。原來 1177155 U 是 I MISS YOU。

繽繽　　　（call 機響）7799——長長久久。

世文　　　（出現在上舞台左後方的光區內）056493358

繽繽　　　哇！世文的每次都 call 這麼長。

　　　　　0564——妳無聊時，93358——就想想我吧！

　　　　　好，我也來 call 他。世文——45，嗯，說什麼呢？

584 520 這樣他放心了嗎？

世文　　（接到）584 520 ——我發誓我愛妳。（一躍到半空中。）

繽繽　　（電話鈴聲）電話鈴響了，會是誰呀？喂， Hello ，もしもし。

錦華　　喂？（原來是媽媽錦華在婚紗店樓下的接待處打電話。）

繽繽　　原來是媽咪呀！

錦華　　喂？妳回來了，不要搞得太晚，貓餵過了沒？

繽繽　　不曉得跑哪裡去了。

錦華　　不想吃就不管牠了。明天要考試，早點睡。

繽繽　　可是我還要跟同學對功課。

錦華　　冰箱裡有雞湯，妳去喝一點，冰淇淋不要吃太多，……（call 機聲）那是什麼聲音？

繽繽　　沒有，我的 call 機在響。

錦華　　是世文，還是瑞琪？

繽繽　　兩個都有，我要回 call 了， bye bye 。

（此起彼落的 call 來 call 去，三人各據舞台一角，有點滑稽，手忙腳亂。）

繽繽	53770880，我想親親妳抱抱妳。討厭，056，
	056。
世文	056，056。她竟然罵我無聊。
繽繽	一直 call 來 call 去累死了，直接三方通話好了。
	（三人打電話）
繽繽	喂？
世文	Hello？
瑞琪	もしもし？
繽繽	你們功課做完在想我呀！
瑞琪	對呀！妳在幹嘛？
繽繽	我在看理化。
瑞琪	還有理化喔？哎喲，我都忘了。繽繽，我剛練了一
	首安室的新歌耶！
繽繽	真的呀？「私は信じです」明天教我們唱。
繽繽	
瑞琪	世文，你在幹嘛？
世文	（故做成熟狀）我在想事情。
瑞琪	我以為你在修你爸爸的老花眼鏡。
世文	不要吐我槽了啦！那妳在幹嘛？
瑞琪	我在看一本詩集。
世文	詩啊，妳聽聽這個：
	有月亮的晚上，童年的夢幻褪色了，不再是只願做

一隻長了翅膀的小精靈。……

繽繽　　　告別童年的宣言。

瑞琪　　　繽繽妳聽聽看：

不再寫流水帳的日記了，換了密密麻麻的模糊的字跡，不對，這是用電腦打的……管他。

在一頁頁深藍淺藍的淚痕裡，有著等待與交心的語句……

繽繽　　　這本我也讀過，我來唸我來唸：如何讓我遇見你，在我最美的時刻，請把我化做一棵樹，在你必經的路旁。……

瑞琪　　　把我化做一棵樹，在你必經的路旁。……

（輕俏浪漫的音樂響起，三人繼續投入地打著電話，音樂聲轉大，燈光漸暗。

音樂連續到下景，在黑暗中，繽繽等三人下。眾 sales 亦把四張桌椅快速的安置在婚紗店內外。）

第七景

（燈光大亮時，音樂轉為歡愉輕快的台灣民謠。）

（婚紗店的攝影師、造型師、經理及 sales 全員出動，招呼著來往眷顧的客人，喜氣洋洋的發揮婚紗攝影的魔法。）

（Sales 婉和造型師 Andy 站在婚紗店內稍右側的 A 桌前，注視著從舞台左上來，邊走邊看的一對男女，男的穿軍服，女的穿套裝，像一位學校老師。）

Sales 婉　　　　怎麼站在門口猶豫呢？要看進來看，沒關係嘛！

造型師 Andy　　歡迎，請進來坐。（客人坐定，sales 婉拿出一些 sample 相簿）

A 桌男客　　　我們只是來看一看，比比價錢。

造型師 Andy　　以中山北路這一帶，我們雖然不是最便宜的，但也不會比別家貴到哪裡。

A 桌女客　　　我們是想多看幾家。

造型師 Andy　　而且，說實在話，比來比去有什麼意思，你們知道你們在比什麼嗎？

（在 A 桌進行時，另一對比較成熟、時髦的男女，從右舞台上，被 sales

勳招呼，坐在較靠近接待處的 B 桌，sales 勳向他們介紹著店中得意的
攝影奇招）

Sales 勳 　　這是我們的 sample，請看：有歐洲式的花園、噴泉
　　　　　　或是原始森林。也有人喜歡比較新奇的，像「恐
　　　　　　龍」、「超人」……

B 桌女客 　　有「酷斯拉」嗎？

Sales 勳 　　啊，哈，哈——當然有，還有「花木蘭」！或是亞
　　　　　　當、夏娃也可以。

B 桌女客 　　這些都是在 studio 裡面拍的嗎？

Sales 勳 　　在我們攝影棚裡拍，效果比出外景還棒。

B 桌男客 　　哦！亞當夏娃穿什麼？

Sales 勳 　　亞當、夏娃的造型比較特別，男生穿一件豹紋短
　　　　　　褲，女生給妳兩個貝殼。

Sales 莉 　　如果你們不能接受這個，我們也有白雪公主搭配七
　　　　　　個小矮人，七個小花童，小紗童。

（B 桌講話暫停，B 桌凝止在半空中。A 桌開始動。）

造型師 Andy 　今天我以私人的角度來看公司，我們公司的造型師
　　　　　　的水準，實在是沒話說。

Sales 婉 　　像 Andy，是中山北路這一帶最紅的造型師。

A 桌女客	嗯……，我有在雜誌上看過。
Sales 婉	你們不覺得他有點面熟？
A 桌女客	（看著造型師 Andy，恍然）啊！就是他。
造型師 Andy	（自信而得意地）婚紗看多了會眼花撩亂，這時候我就能幫你做最好的決定，做最適合你的整體造型。

（他的話尾立刻接上輕俏滑稽的民謠音樂，在這數小節的音樂聲中，接待處左外的 C 桌及最右方樹下的 D 桌都已備妥，D 桌的年輕情侶，也在經理的招呼下入座，各桌的眾 sales 及善男信女，都隨著節拍，誇張的談笑比劃著。音樂一停，D 桌開始談話，其他桌凝止不動。）

經理 Jeff	早上六點，帶妥所有必備的東西，準備出發。
D 桌男客	早上六點？太早了吧！
經理 Jeff	你們如果嫌太早的話，我們還有一個特別的方案。我們公司在大溪有一個專門出外景的山莊。
D 桌女客	是不是鴻禧山莊？
經理 Jeff	嘿嘿，差不多，差不多。 前一天去住，我們會用凱迪拉克載你們去那裡住，第二天就不需要那麼早起出外景。
D 桌男客	喔！真的？凱迪拉克！凱迪拉克！（女客同聲加入歌頌）我們要帶什麼其他的東西嗎？
經理 Jeff	如果不嫌麻煩的話，可以自己帶比較特別，具有紀

念性的禮物呀，第一次約會打的領帶呀……

D 桌女客　　喔！我知道……（親熱的對著男客搥搥打打）

D 桌男客　　第一次做愛的保險套。（女孩尖叫，小腿跨在男友身上。）

（C 桌的客人也已入座，男士穿著老式的西裝，打著領帶，女士穿著洋裝長裙。）

Sales 祥　　你們是從馬來西亞來的？檳城還是沙勞越？

C 桌女客　　檳──

C 桌男客　　城。

Sales 莉　　來我們這裡可就對了，回台灣拍婚紗，可是一生夢幻的實現。

　　　　　　每年春秋兩季，鄰近的國家就會有人組團，特地來台灣拍婚紗。（再用客語加強來台灣拍婚紗）

C 桌男客　　（也用客語）我們兩個是自己組團、兩人成行。

C 桌女客　　（也用客語）我們就是要慢慢逛、慢慢拍。

Sales 祥　　那更好！我們的攝影師是國內外有名聲的，品質更是一大保證！

（A 桌立刻接上）

Sales 婉	對的！我們的攝影師，都是付高薪挖角來的。
造型師 Andy	如果拍出來的照片妳不滿意，可以拍到滿意爲止……
A 桌男客	那你們有重拍的經驗嗎？
Sales 婉	沒有。
造型師 Andy	我看小姐妳這麼漂亮，一定拍什麼都好看。
Sales 婉	你放心，絕對沒問題。（女客對男伴一笑）
	還好你們不是來要贈品的客人，所以我才和你們說
	這些。
造型師 Andy	眞的，不必這麼辛苦再去別家店看什麼了。

（音樂又快速輕俏的響起，眾人熱鬧大動，數小節後，D 桌又開始。）

經理 Jeff	雖然別墅很好玩。但不要玩太晚，少喝水。所以拍
	起照來眼睛才會漂亮。還有，晚上千萬不要興奮過
	度，這樣說你們明白了嗎？
Sales 莉	免得體力耗損，有黑眼圈。（指著自己的眼睛，煽動
	著睫毛，女客也張大嘴巴，摸著自己的眼袋）

（C 桌接續。）

| C 桌女客 | 這兩張都很好看，要挑哪一張呢？ |
| Sales 祥 | 結婚拍婚紗可是女人一輩子永恆的事。所以你們挑 |

照片千萬細心思量，不要挑上自己不滿意的，更重要的是不要放過任何一張。

C 桌女客	可是我們已經挑了三十六張了，再挑就超過一套了。
C 桌男客	是啊！超過一套怎麼辦？
Sales 莉	這有什麼關係呢？多的幾張算妳八折，原本一張八百五。不然這樣好了妳多挑一點，我送妳一本「娘家相本」，專門讓妳送給娘家當紀念。一生只有一次嘛！還是對自己好一點。難得嘛！（又轉為客語，倍加親切地。）
C 桌男客	那就多來幾次嘛！
C 桌女客	（拉著他的領帶）下次你要跟誰來呀？
C 桌男客	當然還是妳囉！（二人做親吻狀，動作凝止。）

（D 桌接續。）

D 桌女客	我們一共拍了三件晚禮服，還有一件中式的，一件日本和服，鞋子有沒有和禮服一起？
經理 Jeff	鞋子是嫁妝的一部分，自己要準備。
D 桌女客	那我還要自己去買呀？
經理 Jeff	鞋子呀！就是和諧，多買幾雙有什麼關係呢？

D 桌男客 D 桌女客	哦！和諧！和諧！
D 桌男客	（體貼的摟著她）明天我先陪妳去買幾雙新鞋。

（B 桌接續。）

B 桌女客	我還是想在結婚當天拍下有紀念性的鏡頭。
Sales 勳	結婚當天拍照，現在很少了啦。
B 桌男客	所以婚紗攝影和結婚是兩回事——？
Sales 勳	告訴妳，結婚是請客，幾十桌客人，吵吵鬧鬧，新娘都看不清楚。拍照才是永久的紀念，一生只有一次，新娘子還是對自己好一點。

（他們站起來，到後牆看禮服。）

（A 桌接續。）

造型師 Andy	我們這家店制度最好，絕對不會中途加價，你可以安心。（客人低頭簽著訂單。）而且，別家請我們的攝影師去拍照做 sample ， sample 雖好，成品就差了。
Sales 婉	真正差的成品其實是在客人家裡，我們敢讓你看毛片，而且這些還是客人挑剩下的呢。

造型師 Andy　　別家難看的不會讓你看的！

（音樂又響起了數小節，經理 Jeff 來回走動，盡最大的努力。）

經理 Jeff　　你們知道嗎？才幾萬元的生意，真的是為新人服務啦，妳來預約、訂婚挑衣服、拿衣服、拍照前溝通、拍照、挑婚禮的禮服、拿衣服、看片、拿片，一個 case 才一千、兩千的抽紅，不用擔心，有緣分就相信我，就交給婚紗店。

（客人簽單雙雙攜手而去，經理 Jeff 開始收拾東西。）
（C 桌接續。）

C 桌男客　　那底片呢？我們住的這麼遠，檳城呢！（又轉為客語）想要再加洗的話，還要再坐飛機飛回來，多麻煩。

C 桌女客　　這樣子好了，你們再送我們幾張底片怎麼樣？

Sales 祥　　嗯……這個……我想，是沒有別家店在送的，但是我可以想辦法跟經理商量看看。（走過去對經理 Jeff 作商量狀）經理，怎麼樣？（再滿臉笑容轉身對客人說）我看你們這麼大老遠跑來，而且我們又這麼有緣，應該是可以送給你們幾張的啦。

C 桌男客　　　（大悅，充滿手勢的說）這樣子我們就可以回家 DIY
　　　　　　　啦！

（B 桌的客人，簽了訂單，交還給 sales 勳，並慢慢走向婚紗店的門
外。）

Sales 勳　　　我們婚紗攝影一年漲價兩次，這就是爲什麼新人都
　　　　　　　提早下訂單。現在下訂單眞是划算，兩年後就可以
　　　　　　　省兩、三萬。
B 桌女客　　　（站在門口，回頭說）世界上眞的有這種又浪漫，又
　　　　　　　划算的事嗎？
造型師 Andy　（一面收東西，一面湊趣的加入）當然有了！
Sales 勳　　　而且妳知道嗎？趕公元兩千年、千禧年結婚的一大
　　　　　　　堆。妳這位最有氣質的新娘，今天可是做了最聰明
　　　　　　　的選擇。

（女客牽著男子的手，輕快地從右舞台出去。）
（台上只剩下這群信心十足、神采自若的 sales，順手安置桌椅，整理店
中的擺飾。）

Sales 祥　　　雖然外國的時裝走在時代的尖端，但是談到這個婚
　　　　　　　紗啊，就比不上我們台灣，台灣的婚紗是世界第一

流的，談到結婚禮服，外國就不行了。

Sales 莉　　　現在大陸的婚紗店也在學台北，北京就有一家「台灣婚紗店」，上海也有，都是台商去帶動的，簡直賺翻了。

造型師 Andy　還有成都，我堂哥開的。

Sales 祥　　　其實，台北的婚紗攝影才是眞正的（造型師 Andy 等加入幫腔）「台灣經驗」呢！

（音樂拉起，強有力的結尾，他們瞬間轉入後台，燈光轉換。）

第八景

（外婆君美和她的好友阿梅，抱著各色禮服舞裙由舞台左側慢慢走上，
觀眾聽到裴裴對她們喊話。）

裴裴　　　　阿媽，我去停車，妳衣服抱不抱得動？

外婆君美　　（也回頭大聲說）我沒問題，再多都抱得動。本來是
　　　　　　要搭伊的歐多拜來的。

裴裴　　　　眞的，這麼厲害。

姨婆阿梅　　沒什麼啦！上次去新莊——藝文中心——都是我騎
　　　　　　車去的。

外婆君美　　還有汐止——（轉身向外，更大聲的喊）我們在這裡
　　　　　　等妳。

（兩位老太太抱著衣服，小聲商量。）

外婆君美　　妳說他們會不會不肯幫我們改？

姨婆阿梅　　不會啦，上次就改過一件，不會不肯啦。
　　　　　　景氣不好，（更有把握的說）今年又是孤鸞年，那有
　　　　　　那麼多人結婚，生意不好做，一定什麼錢都肯賺。

外婆君美　　　好啊，先去跟他們講看看。（裝出現，快步走過來幫

外婆拿手中的衣物等。）

裴裴，你相片怎麼那麼快好？

裴裴　　　　不是，我先來看，我不要媽媽又跟來了。妳不要跟

她講哦。

外婆君美　　（兩位老太太會心一笑）跟她講幹什麼。

（兩人跟在裴裴後面，往店裡走。）

姨婆阿梅　　妳是有拍那種很限制級的，「不搭不七」的？

外婆君美　　有的話借我們看，沒關係。

裴裴　　　　阿媽，不是啦。是……

（在阿媽耳邊說悄悄話，阿梅故意湊過去聽，兩人驚奇互看，並且怪

笑。）

姨婆阿梅　　眞的、眞的喔！

（三人一起進去，店員把毛片捧出來給她們看。）

姨婆阿梅　　（台語）這兩個看起來攏不壞，一個緣投，那個較古

意也較古錐。

外婆君美	（台語）妳是不是不歡喜妳老母揀的那一個？
裴裴	也不是啦。阿媽，查某囝子是不是攏一定要結婚？
外婆君美	（故意拉出歌仔戲的調子）這……
姨婆阿梅	這……（也作歌仔戲小生搓手拍頭狀）
外婆君美	這我不敢和妳黑白講，妳阿母要生氣。結婚嘛，是有較好。
姨婆阿梅	結婚嘛，如果眼睛睜大點是有較好。
外婆君美	有的時候外表看不出來。
姨婆阿梅	有的人結婚以前脾氣都很好，結婚以後就都很不好。
外婆君美	找妳自己適合的嫁就好。
姨婆阿梅	找不到就免嫁。

（外婆君美突然看到店中化妝架上，假人頭所戴的假髮。）

外婆君美	這個假髮和我從小剪的那個頭髮很像。
Sales 祥	（把假髮取下，幫君美試戴）你要不要戴戴看？
姨婆阿梅	（還在桌上，對兩位男友品頭論足）看妳這兩個男朋友，妳都不要，不會吧？
	不要還來拍這種妖嬌美麗、情投意合的照片，是想給什麼人看？
裴裴	阿媽，妳為什麼要嫁給阿公？

Sales 祥	這是你阿媽，真是好福氣喲！
	（指著一套式樣特殊的中古衣裙）
	請您幫我們試裝。
裴裴	（與阿媽走進梳妝換衣之處）阿媽，妳結婚是幾歲？
外婆君美	我，（已戴上假髮，像日本時代女學生的髮型——妹妹頭）
	作女孩子的時候，怎麼都沒想到要結婚。
	我讀完公學校，就想要報考中學。那時台灣只有一所給台灣女孩子讀的高等中學「第三高女」，我後來就考上了。
Sales 婉	第三高女是哪一個學校？
Sales 莉	中山女高。
姨婆阿梅	她很威風呢，一直都擔任舍長。
	理科、算數永遠是一百分。鋼琴、畫畫，還有賽跑也第一名。畢業的時候校長還以為她會去日本念醫學院。

（此時外婆君美已經換好當時流行的女學生服裝，米色小花，旗袍領，唐裝上衣，百褶裙，清純素雅，接待處的窗口已嵌好窗欄景片，在燈光下，可映出日式的風味。）

外婆君美	但是，（往前走，獨自一人，其他人都在老遠望著她）

	高中畢業，就有很多大戶人家請媒人上門提親，這張文憑，讓我變成一個更有身價的待嫁娘。
Sales 婉	那時候聘金也是很講究，第三高女六千金、靜修女中三千金、職業學校兩千金、連公學校畢業也起碼一千金。
Sales 祥	不止，一萬金兩萬金多的是。
外婆君美	只是我很傷心……（慢慢抬起頭，彷彿對著校長。校長身穿日本時代的校長制服，戴帽子，出現在舞台左後方光圈下。）校長，我想……讀醫科。
校長	（日本式的語氣）君美樣，讀醫科，嗯，妳的成績是不錯的，目前在台灣，女孩子讀醫學院還不能夠，我想到時候我可以給妳寫介紹信到日本去，先接受兩年的化學訓練，打好基礎，再申請東京女子醫科專門學校。
	啊——，妳家裡有辦法出錢讓妳去日本讀嗎？
外婆君美	我母親早已過世，我二媽媽不會捨得給我去，我父親也不會肯……
	（低頭不語）
校長	喔——，這樣子……那畢業以後……要做什麼？（沒等到君美的答案，就嘆了一口氣）我本來以為……沒彩！（搖搖頭，慢慢消失）
外婆君美	我回絕了上門來提親的那些人家，我自己和一個同

學的堂哥交往，他寫給我的信，我都拿給我父親看過。（開始口氣和姿態輕鬆起來，猶如回到少女時代。）

父親很生氣，但我不肯理那些有錢人家的男孩，怕這樣的人談不來或是品格不好，最後我說我不要嫁妝，家人讓步了。

（她坐在接待處的明式椅上，sales 祥口啣一根長線，為她挽臉。）

Sales 婉　　那時候已經有人用西洋的婚紗了，妳穿怎樣的？

外婆君美　　我就穿這樣的，圍一條水紅色的紗巾，帶著一對我二媽給我的鴛鴦枕頭和一籃雞蛋，就從父親家走到丈夫家了。

（Sales 莉把一塊暗紅色的紗巾披在外婆君美的肩上。）

Sales 祥　　嗄，真的嗎？沒有吹吹打打，也沒有花轎迎接，妳就這樣走過去，這怎麼算真心要娶新娘呢？

Sales 莉　　這話也不是這樣講的啦！只是很奇怪，想不到阿媽那時候還蠻新派的嘛！

Sales 婉　　好可惜，否則說不一定現在還可以看到阿媽的結婚照，那種古老相片看過沒有？禮服很特別，髮型也是……

裴裴　　　　阿媽，妳有沒有後悔？

外婆君美　　（在女孩子們討論中，她已走到舞台前）能夠這樣結
　　　　　　婚，我是不會後悔的，能夠等到雙方家長答應，等
　　　　　　了很久，實在不容易。不過，結了婚，自己想做什
　　　　　　麼事都不能做，生活很辛苦，大多不如意，都想自
　　　　　　己當初怎麼那麼傻……，阿公也一樣。

（她往舞台前左光區望去，年輕時代的阿公穿著黃卡其中山裝，跪坐在
地板上。他把手上的書闔上，筆插回口袋。）

阿公　　　　我只要文學，不要小孩。

外婆君美　　我剛一聽，嚇了一跳。

阿公　　　　一個都不生大概不行吧，先生一個好了。

外婆君美　　我就知道上當了。

阿公　　　　要是個女孩，就再生一個，生到第三個再說。

外婆君美　　三個都是女孩，不能叫我再生男孩。

阿公　　　　到時候妳再決定吧。

外婆君美　　（在回憶中敘述著）那時候的男人肯在結婚之前討論
　　　　　　這樣的事，算不錯了。誰知道他後來都耍賴說……

阿公　　　　這妳怎麼能怪我，當初又沒有寫明、蓋章、證明什
　　　　　　麼的，（外婆君美微慍的把臉轉開，阿公挨過去靠在
　　　　　　她肩上。）妳說的時候我都有同意，我還以為到時

候……唉，我也不知道，妳會那麼容易，我是說，我們會那麼容易，這樣生……（阿公整個頭都靠著君美。君美默默不語，然後愛憐地伸出手掌，拂著他的臉。）

外婆君美　我那時候也想過要「避」，可是避不來，以前不像現在，孩子一年一年出生，我什麼都忘光光了。（外婆君美漸漸站起）彈琴？畫畫？十隻纖纖手指磨成枯樹枝。

只有結婚那一天是新派、是進步的，以爲在效法什麼革命。（把身上的披肩取下來，在手中扭轉著）後來才知道養孩子、洗衣服、洗尿布、生火、煮飯……，唉，那時候生活苦，大人小孩都容易生病，每一個孩子都不好帶，唉……

（手中的布巾轉成襁褓模樣，她抱在懷中拍哄著，阿公也站起來關切的看著她。然後接過手中的襁褓。「搖嬰仔歌」的音樂響起，兩人一同走往婚紗店方向。店中的 sales 一一忙著手中的事物，而「嬰仔」傳到眼前時，又轉入另一種時空，小心翼翼的把「嬰仔」抱過來，傳給下一位，直傳到上舞台最後的那一位，再抱出去。君美靜立。音樂漸停。）

（繽繽和世文從舞台右下走出沿著舞台前緣邊走邊說，說完正好從舞台左下消失。）

| 繽繽 | 那時候的醫藥、衛生、營養以及遺傳科學都很不健全，我外婆生了十一胎，天啊！好累啊。 |
| | 到現在，她只剩第三、第七和第十一還在。我媽媽是第七，唯一的女兒，更不可能送給別人做養女，而且不管多辛苦都讓我媽唸書，唸最好的學校，比兩個舅舅都讀得高。 |

（外婆君美已回到婚紗店內，正在脫假髮。）

外婆君美	現在不一樣，大兒子還生了三個，女兒兩個，小兒子只要一個，攏好。
Sales 莉	現在都有計畫，我們這一行婚紗攝影的都會把淡季、旺季先算好來生小孩。
Sales 婉	（自顧自的說話）而且在婚紗店的同事最近都想生女兒，好像生女兒的也比較多。
Sales 祥	會嗎？大家每天看到這些漂亮的禮服，心都變柔軟了。
Sales 婉	還是做女生佔便宜，不管那個男生長得多帥、多有地位、多有錢，大家看的還是只有新娘。
Sales 莉	我真的很高興我從事的是這種「美的行業」。
外婆君美	（在三位 sales 的幫助下，外婆君美已換回原來的衣服，往前走向裝裝和阿梅）這個女孩子一定要給她有自己

的前途，有能力就要多做，不能結了婚，靠先生，沒有意思。

裴裴　　阿媽，那妳是不是覺得晚婚比較好？還是不要結婚？

外婆君美　（矢口否認）沒有，我沒有說晚婚，也沒有說不結婚。

姨婆阿梅　妳們可以去結，我們（指外婆與自己）不用再結啦！

（繽繽和友伴出現在舞台左前方。）

瑞琪　　生孩子太可怕了，現在很多人都說不要生小孩。

繽繽　　可是沒有人生，就沒有我們。

瑞琪　　但是那麼痛怎麼辦，其實領養也可以，領養的和親生的沒有什麼差別。

世文　　如果有一個小孩和自己長的很像，譬如有妳的眉毛、眼睛，嗯，嘴唇、鼻子和妳們的臉頰不是更好嗎？難道妳們不喜歡嗎？

瑞琪　　喜歡。繽繽，那還是要親生的，那要怎麼辦？

世文　　其實科學那麼發達，一定有辦法讓生孩子不痛。

繽繽　　也許可以用試管嬰兒，但是還是要人去生出來，對了，基因複製。

瑞琪　　基因複製就是做一個和自己一模一樣的。就不能像

	妳又像我。
世文	還要像我。
瑞琪	056 ─ 056 ─
世文	像我也沒有什麼不好，我是說也有像繽繽，也有像妳，難道就沒有辦法像三個人嗎？
繽繽	我認為一定有。
	我去找找看我媽媽的書架上有沒有講這些東西的文章，說不定人類已經在發明了。
	（三個人蹦跳而下。）

（君美重新整理好頭髮，成為現在的阿媽樣子。）

外婆君美	謝謝妳們剛才的恭維，我那套衣服好看對不對？妳們不是也列入中古款式之一。
Sales 婉	當然好看，只是沒想到會真的有人在結婚當天穿。
	（話鋒一轉，對君美深深一鞠躬）
	感謝您給我們試裝，我會告訴以後來拍照的新娘，這套衣服的穿著方式和當時的時代應有的氣質。
姨婆阿梅	（台語）啊──，妳講那麼久，都沒講到這些衣服。
外婆君美	（大笑）對啦！啊，我啊癡呆症了！小姐，這些舊的衣服，麻煩你改，不用改，只要放大，放很大，

我們歐巴桑可以穿就好了。

Sales 莉   這是妳要穿的嗎？

外婆君美   我們是長青團隊啦！國際標準舞長青團隊。

姨婆阿梅   最近要籌備出國比賽，想先穿這樣來練習用。這是獅子會捐贈的，不用錢，所以妳們修改也算少一點。

裴裴   說不定他們出國比賽的正式舞裙會在妳們這裡訂做。

Sales 莉   好吧。那請妳們拿到三樓後面那間去跟師傅講修改的事。

外婆君美
姨婆阿梅   好好，謝謝，真的謝謝，好，願意改就好⋯⋯

（兩人抱著大堆衣裙往後走。）

（繽繽和友伴出現在舞台左後方，手中都抱著大本的書籍資料，在翻閱著。）

瑞琪   那兩個女的可不可以？

繽繽   可以，只要把兩個受精卵的胚胎結合就行了。

瑞琪   那兩個男的可不可以？

繽繽   那⋯⋯應該也可以。

世文   那兩個女的和一個男的可不可以？

繽繽	當然可以囉！本來就是要一個精子和兩個卵子。
世文	那誰要懷孕？

（兩個女孩互看，緊張的氣氛出現。然後繽繽用肘彎撞撞瑞琪。）

繽繽	妳好了。
瑞琪	（也去撞繽繽）妳好了。
繽繽	（更親密地）妳好了。
瑞琪	（也磨著她）妳好了。
世文	（被冷落在一旁，突發奇想）那我好了。（兩個女孩瞪著他看） 我願意呀！如果我可以的話。

（兩個女孩準備衝過去 K 他，繽繽把手中的書往瑞琪懷裡一丟，開始追打世文，瑞琪跟在後面跑，三人衝出左上的門，往右邊的巷道奔去，只見繽繽一躍，跳上世文的背，三人奔跑遠去。）

第九景

（台上只剩'下裴裴。燈光昏暗，氣氛詭異。裴裴斜掛在椅子上，頭歪腿斜。突然把高跟鞋踢掉。）

裴裴　　　　阿媽，妳們自己都說不肯再結了，再也不結了，為什麼我要結？

（裴裴突然站起來）

結婚就不能再做自己的事了。（翻開桌上疊得高高的相片簿）

結婚就再也沒有戀愛的感覺了。（翻著那些相片，啼笑皆非）

結婚就是每天一成不變的生活。（雙手捧起那一疊燙金的相簿，不知道是那般厚重，幾乎跌倒）

結婚就是要和心愛的人在一起。（捧著厚重的相簿，歪歪倒倒的往外走）

十年、二十年、三十年……，除非……（見到媽媽錦華奔過去）

媽，好可怕，好恐怖，我真是想起來就受不了，太恐怖啦！

錦華	發生什麼事？怎麼了？
裴裴	（變回鎮定的模樣）我只是在想，我只是在想，我只是……，我不敢想……，我只是……語無倫次。

（小周和 Tony 各自穿著拍照時的禮服，出現在接待處的窗框後，擺好姿勢，宛如巨大的相片。）

錦華	（指著 Tony 又指著小周）是因為他使妳語無倫次？還是因為他？
裴裴	不。是因為我自己，也是因為妳。
錦華	不要怪到我身上，妳什麼時候長大成熟到不要什麼都怪到媽媽身上，妳就可以結婚了。（突覺失言）
小周	裴裴真浪漫。
Tony	裴裴真聰明。
小周	我就是要娶這種女孩子，又能幹，又可愛，就像我的丈母娘。
Tony	哈，哈，哈，就像丈母娘。
裴裴	妳聽到沒有？（站在她母親身後問）
錦華	（平靜的面朝前說）我們努力了一輩子，

（太婆秀貞悠然自屏風後出現，姿態年輕、可愛；外婆君美從婚紗店樓上下來，對禮服東張西望了一下，站定，秀貞看著君美，君美面朝前，

看著錦華，錦華看著台中徬徨的裴裴。巨大相片般的小周和 Tony 消失。）

錦華　　　　就是希望我們的女兒，不要再像我們那樣⋯⋯

（裴裴抬頭看著母親，錦華拾起裴裴的高跟鞋，往裴裴的方向走去，裴裴退後，兩人往左邊離場。秀貞亦飄然消失。剩下外婆君美提著「獨身貴族」的大紙袋漸漸離開婚紗店。）

（音樂突然轉換成輕快而明亮，舞台燈光也大亮，一對對情侶顧客按著節拍湧上舞台，和 sales 交叉穿梭，熱絡的討論，興奮的比畫，在舞蹈和默劇的進行中，散發婚紗店浪漫的魔法。）

（這段無聲戲的高潮是一位試裝的新娘，由左上角跌跌撞撞進來，她穿著過高的鞋子，踩到過長的裙擺，當眾翻滾跌倒在舞台正中。造型師 Andy 趕快去扶她起來，她掙扎地站好，卻又倒地一次。眾人驚笑，幕急落。）

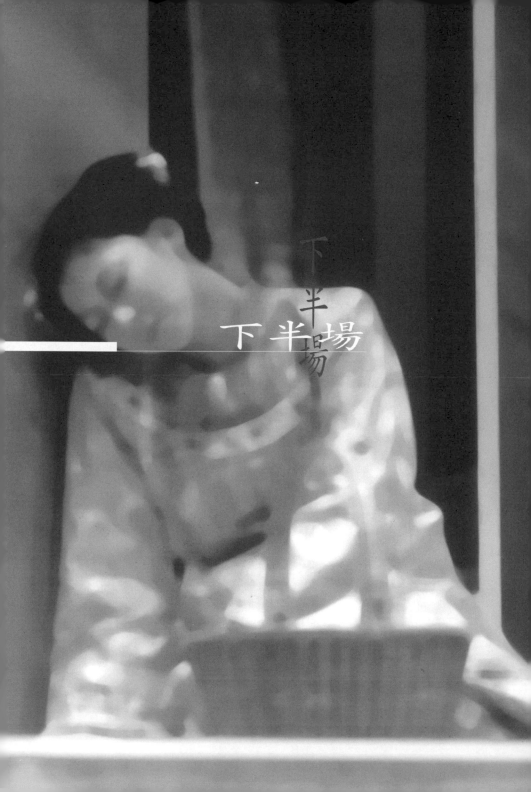

下半場

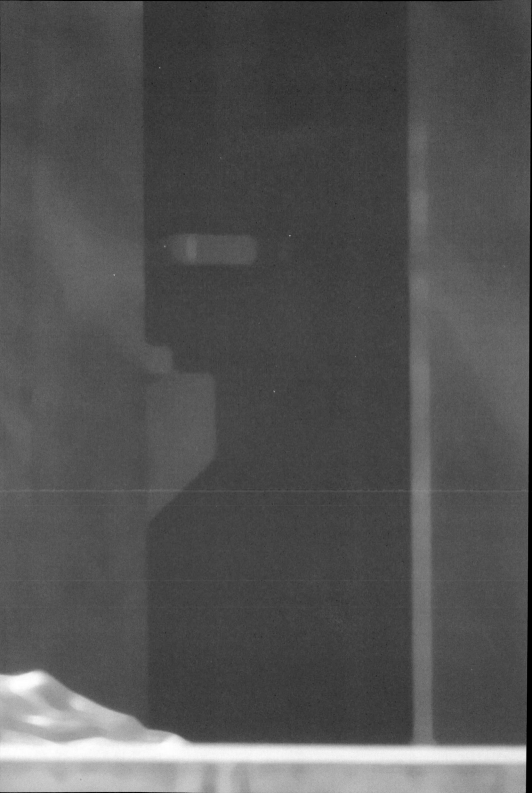

第一景

（幕起時，史特勞斯圓舞曲演奏著，一對對舞者的剪影，在樂聲中搖晃，燈亮後，看到的是一對對阿公阿媽在跳華爾滋。君美的舞伴是男裝的阿梅，她們送去修改的舞裙，也都穿在老太太們的身上。有一位教練也在阿公阿媽的交叉迴旋中，頻頻發出口令，一不小心，有兩對相撞。）

阿公甲　　　哎喲喂呀！

外婆君美　　金元，你有沒有怎樣？教練，讓我們休息一下，喝口水。

阿公乙　　　唉，不要休息，等一下打太極拳的那些老伙仔來了，就要讓場地了。

阿婆甲　　　對不起，是我跳錯，下次會記住。

教練　　　　下次就來不及了，下次就要在里民大會表演了。

阿婆甲　　　喔！真的。

外婆君美　　那不是還有退休人聯誼會？

姨婆阿梅　　那是下個月五號，下個月啦！

阿公甲　　　（重聽）什麼啊？

外婆君美 姨婆阿梅	退休人聯誼會啦！

（同時大聲喊，阿公甲聽見了，張著嘴大大點頭）

姨婆阿梅	不過也快了。
阿公甲	對了，那阿美，妳的孫女結婚不是要我們去表演，是講真的還是講假的？
外婆君美	真的啊。
阿公丙	那是什麼時候？
外婆君美	時間她還沒定。
阿婆甲	不是已經拍結婚照，相都已經拍好，怎麼還不知道什麼時候結婚，是不想和妳講還是怎樣？
阿婆乙	說不定是不想要我們歐巴桑去表演不好意思講，就說沒有決定。
姨婆阿梅	不會啦，不會啦。現在年輕的女孩都很忙碌，沒時間。
外婆君美	我想她大概真的是很難決定的樣子。
姨婆阿梅	我去幫妳們問好了，作阿媽的自己問，又有「壓力」了啦！
教練	阿公、阿媽，不要再聊天了！我們再來練啦！我們再來練一次，你們最喜歡的探戈（示範幾個動作，眾人驚嘆），美美的，身體滑出去，來，音樂。我們這樣一直跳，跳到那邊去，那邊比較大。

（阿公阿媽成雙成對的，有板有眼的跳著探戈，有的跟不上拍子，有的扭得漂亮極了，長青團隊趣味橫生，由舞台左邊，邊跳邊出場。

探戈的尾音，轉變成略帶淒清的音樂，戶外的燈光轉變成婚紗店的室內照明。）

第二景

（造型師 Andy 獨自坐在桌前看雜誌，sales 婉悶悶的走上來，欲言又止。）

Sales 婉　　　我想跟你講一件事情，你不要跟別人講好不好？真的不要跟別人說。

造型師 Andy　不能跟別人說？（對八卦極感興趣，卻又開玩笑）完了，不會是要向我借錢吧？又被倒會啦？

Sales 婉　　　不要這樣子，人家要跟你好好講話，你就這樣鬧我（捶他），不要跟你講了，討厭。

造型師 Andy　好啦，好啦！快點。（等半天）怎麼啦？（忍不住又開玩笑）妳又懷孕了？

（Sales 婉真的生氣，白眼瞪他，不講。）

造型師 Andy　好，（作發誓狀）不開玩笑。

Sales 婉　　　我想，再做半個月，有朋友要找我，一起去開……個人工作室。

造型師 Andy　哈，又是哪裡的朋友？

Sales 婉	就是以前學服裝設計時候的朋友。
造型師 Andy	妳想自己出去做？
Sales 婉	也不是啦！上個月的業績做不到一百萬。
造型師 Andy	最近這幾個月，是比較難，客人也精打細算，大家都覺得壓力蠻大的。
Sales 婉	經理是沒說什麼，我自己很不好意思。每次看客人進來，又眼睜睜地看客人走出去，費盡唇舌，下單都下不成，我心裡就急得只差沒有拿刀架在客人的脖子上。
造型師 Andy	做哪一行沒有起起落落，唉，妳，不要以為出去做很容易，很多人自己當老闆，倒了，不都跑回來做 sales，我自己也回鍋過一次啊。 台灣的婚紗店倒的比開的還多，真的，妳不要急著走，再試試看嘛！
Sales 婉	唉，再下去，我就真的要跟你借錢了，（惡意開自己玩笑）比懷孕容易。

（造型師 Andy 拍她，盡力安慰。）

Sales 勳	（匆匆由左跑上）抱歉，sorry，sorry，阿浩不能來上班，胃出血，我剛送他去醫院。
Sales 婉	怎麼搞到胃出血？

Sales 勳	他晚上都去兼差幫人拍廣告，胃痛都不管。
造型師 Andy	怎麼，都不要命了，白天晚上做兩個工怎麼行。
Sales 勳	我還不是也要兼差，否則怎麼辦，老婆孩子跟著我喝西北風呀？
	不過我不能像阿浩那樣白天晚上到處亂跑，我只能在家裡對著電腦做完稿，抓 mouse 抓得手腕都僵了。
Sales 婉	（怪笑）怪不得你拍出來的片子都有「動感效果」。
Sales 勳	不要再損我了，我都被小師傅 K 了好幾次。所以我才勸人家不要太早結婚。
Sales 婉	噓——，婚紗店不能講。
Sales 勳	什麼不能講，事實本來就是這樣。錢歹賺，子細漢，某不繪賺……
Sales 婉	自己就不要怨嘆！（拍拍 sales 勳安慰，隨即嘆了一口氣。）
	誰知道阿浩，想結婚想瘋了。
造型師 Andy	阿浩不是跟他那個女朋友已經很穩了，他們不是一起住在景美？
Sales 勳	對啦！以前學校旁邊，從五專住到現在。
造型師 Andy	那很好啊！跟結婚有什麼差別。
Sales 婉	他們兩個都在拚命存錢，買了房子才可以結婚啊。
造型師 Andy	爲什麼？

Sales 婉　　　這樣才比較安定，免得家裡人又有話說、囉里巴嗦。

（Sales 莉從店內出來）

Sales 莉　　　唉呀，好可憐呀！有了房子又怎麼樣。（有感而發，拭淚）

Sales 婉　　　妳怎麼啦？妳老公又不回家了？（sales 莉點頭）幾天了？

Sales 莉　　　他最近七、八天沒回來了，只打過電話回來過一次，說他不能回家，因爲那個女的會拿菜刀自殺。

Sales 婉　　　哎喲！搞什麼呀？

Sales 勳　　　那種老公不要算了！

造型師 Andy　他怎麼都不怕妳拿菜刀啊？妳也去鬧嘛！到他辦公室去，拿菜刀去，眞的，小婉，妳陪她去。

Sales 婉　　　幹嘛？爲什麼你不陪她去？

造型師 Andy　我去會被誤會啦。

Sales 婉　　　應該是（瞄他一眼）不會啦！

造型師 Andy　會說啦！來來來，不要哭不要哭，把眼睛哭腫了怎麼辦？等一下客人進來還以爲我們發生了什麼事。

Sales 莉　　　好啦！沒有啦，沒有啦！（擦去眼淚，又做出甜美的聲音）不管我們自己的遭遇怎麼樣，我們還是要祝福來結婚的新人。

Sales 婉　　妳不要太難過，等會兒我早點下班，我陪妳一起去
　　　　　接娃娃，然後再帶她去吃披薩。
　　　　　今天有好幾組客人要看片，先去整理出來吧！（拍
　　　　　著她的肩膀，一起到後面工作。）

造型師 Andy　今天怎麼搞的，那麼多人不來上班，你們兩個又想
　　　　　早下班，那我也去游個泳好了。阿勳，你一個人唱
　　　　　獨腳戲吧。

Sales 勳　　不會只剩我一個人吧？小武也沒來？上哪兒去啦？
　　　　　他還在等照片嗎？

Sales 莉　　那是急件，他昨天已經拿回來了。

Sales 婉　　所以，他今天是跟經理去開世貿婚紗展的籌備會
　　　　　囉？

造型師 Andy　沒有沒有，Jeff 是自己開車去的。

Sales 勳　　那小武到底上哪裡去啦？啊！我知道了。他有說過
　　　　　要去公證結婚，說不定就是今天。

Sales 婉　　今天？公證結婚？不會吧？

造型師 Andy　哎喲！真是的，怎麼搞的。怎麼大家都不知道啊？

Sales 婉　　真不夠意思，講都不講一聲。

Sales 莉　　不是講好員工價四折嗎？為什麼不在店裡結呢？我
　　　　　們也不會賺他的錢。

Sales 婉　　（怪笑）很難說。

Sales 勳	（戲謔地）而且皺紋也很難修。
造型師 Andy	（更渲染的）修了就可以放在門口做 sample 了。
Sales 婉	但是我還是不相信他會自己溜去結婚，他說他不會結婚。
造型師 Andy	說說而已吧，嘴上越說不想結婚的越結得快。妳別這樣橫眉豎眼的，反正他一定會出現，這錢他扣不起，這個月已經超休了。
Sales 婉	（長嘆一聲）好吧，我總不能跟所有沒有在我們店裡結婚的人過不去。

第三景

（婚紗店的人還在上段戲的哀嘆的基調的餘波中，沒精打彩整理店中的東西，裴裴從舞台左邊出現，往店中走來，Andy 一看到她，馬上揚聲招呼。）

造型師 Andy　　哈囉！妳好！

（兩位女 sales 也立時收起愁容，轉身對顧客做出開朗的笑臉。）

Sales 婉　　裴裴小姐，妳的相片都好了。（拍一下 sales 莉示意）

Sales 莉　　都在這裡，來，我拿給妳看。每一張都很漂亮，拍
　　　　　　得很成功，攝影助理都說，很少有這麼沒有瑕疵的
　　　　　　case。

裴裴　　喔？真的嗎？連我跌倒的樣子都能看嗎？

Sales 莉　　好可愛喔！

（裴裴認真的看著自己的相片，Tony 從後面巷道過來，一路吹著口哨在婚紗店外停止腳步，卻以口哨的暗號呼叫裴裴。）

（裴裴回頭看見 Tony，開心的拿著相片往外奔。）

裴裴	Tony，你提早回來了？（她投入 Tony 懷中，Tony 將她抱起轉了一圈。）
Tony	提早一兩天，我有事情告訴妳。
裴裴	好事還是壞事？車被吊走了，要我去拿回來？信用卡被偷了？護照不見了？
Tony	都不是，我有那麼「天兵」就好了。告訴妳，一好一壞，我先講壞的。（變聲調，故作哀慟狀）我戒煙了。

（裴裴忍不住大笑，Tony 繼續歌頌自己。）

Tony	戒煙，剝奪了我的一切。 尤其是和幻覺相關的樂趣：姿態——手勢——眼神——風味——，遺世而獨立——，還有，死不改過。 但是，重新使我變成「周恩來」，一天只需要睡四小時，而且還可以踢一場足球。
裴裴	真是 tough choice。 哎呀，這是壞的，好的呢？
Tony	那個 case 過了，我們工作室是第二名，其實會跟第一名合併，所以……
裴裴	兩百八十萬……（Tony 搖頭）五百？厲害，怪不得

你說戒煙是壞的。

（兩人親膩的貼著臉，一起坐在左邊樹下的花台聊天。）
（另一端舞台右下角，出現媽媽錦華和小周。）

小周　　　「家母」其實很急，只是不好意思催，她疼裴裴，
　　　　　所以連帶對我這個做兒子也客氣起來，拐彎抹角要
　　　　　我姊姊來問我，還說連房子都幫我們準備好了。
　　　　　家母很喜歡裴裴，裴裴到台南，家母就巴不得天天
　　　　　請客，讓親戚朋友都來看她。
　　　　　最近她還把家裡的沙發都換過一套，就是……爲了
　　　　　……到時候，請妳們下去……請客的時候有面子。

錦華　　　哎，這眞是過意不去，也眞感心咧！你對裴裴，我
　　　　　是沒話講，她自己怎麼計畫，我是不知道。一下子
　　　　　像大人，一下子又像小孩，有你照顧那也放心。
　　　　　可是，她好像什麼事情放不下。

小周　　　女孩子嘛，想到離開爸爸媽媽的家會害怕，會捨不
　　　　　得，我會耐心等她。不是說什麼（以下用台語說出這
　　　　　個追求老婆的俗諺）又要好膽，又要皮，又要跪要
　　　　　拜。

錦華　　　「六好膽，七皮，八綿……」
　　　　　你也聽過這個，怎麼說的，我想一想，是這樣的：

「一錢，二緣，三水，四少年，」

這你都不壞呀！

五，五是什麼？

小周	「五敢」。
錦華	「五敢」。
兩人同聲	「六好膽，七皮，八綿，九跪，十拜。」

（準丈母娘被小周逗得開心大笑。）

（錦華和小周這區的燈光轉暗，另一角的裴裴和 Tony 又亮起。）

裴裴	有時候覺得安定下來的感覺很奇怪，每天每天過一樣的日子。
Tony	跟我在一起，白天和晚上一定不一樣。
裴裴	你呀，白天睡覺，晚上去 pub。
Tony	你太抬舉我了，白天也在 pub。不對，這也太抬舉我了，我忙得像狗一樣，起碼一個月有七、八天不睡覺，也不去 pub。剩下的時候，（聲調溫柔）妳都知道，都在妳的監督之下。
裴裴	才沒有呢！（回頭親 Tony 一下，也充滿柔情，二人相偎。） 妳會不會永遠這樣愛我？
Tony	會愛妳，

裴裴　　　　但是……

Tony　　　　不會一模一樣的愛，我是變化無窮的。

裴裴　　　　那我是詭計多端的。

Tony　　　　就像這些照片。

（裴裴把相片取出和 Tony 一起翻看，自然的往前走幾步，就著路燈的
光挑選。）

裴裴　　　　妳喜歡我們的相片？

　　　　　　喜歡哪一張？

Tony　　　　這張。

裴裴　　　　Me too！我也最喜歡這張。

Tony　　　　我不是不想娶妳，總有一天，我們會有一種最完整
　　　　　　的親密，百分百無形的，像共同擁有一個精神的城
　　　　　　堡。
　　　　　　現在，還有點難，（裴裴開始有點距離）妳再等一陣
　　　　　　子，好不好？（他斜眼看她）妳不會去嫁那個戴
　　　　　　POLO 眼鏡、打 YSL 領帶、在新竹科學園區上班的
　　　　　　……

裴裴　　　　他媽媽逼得很緊——。

Tony　　　　妳又不是和他家人結婚——。

裴裴　　　　他在我媽面前下的功夫很多！

Tony　　　　好賤！這太下流了吧。

（裴裴哈哈大笑。）
（燈光轉換）

小周　　　　皮，棉，跪，拜都歸我，不過她願意來拍婚紗，其
　　　　　　實是裴裴建議的，我想也好，就像那個 sales 說
　　　　　　的，婚期不遠了。
　　　　　　今天麻煩伯母來，幫裴裴挑幾張特別美的，然後再
　　　　　　決定真正要穿的那件白紗禮服。我想裴裴會想要訂
　　　　　　做一套全新的。

錦華　　　　我想是，你們兩個賺錢也不容易。我跟她爸爸說好
　　　　　　了，要是拍全套的，還有出外景什麼的，一定花費
　　　　　　不少，十一、二萬少不了吧？我們兩老來出吧。

小周　　　　不用，千萬不用你們兩位費心。

錦華　　　　我和她爸都講好了。

小周　　　　伯母，不信裴裴一定也這樣說。

（兩人相持著，往婚紗店去。）

Tony　　　　來，我們去加洗那張相片。

（他們倆也一起往婚紗店走。）

（於是母親錦華、小周，裴裴、 Tony ，四人相遇在門口。）

錦華　　　　這是怎麼回事？

Tony　　　　這是怎麼回事？

小周　　　　這是怎麼回事？

裴裴　　　　這是怎麼回事？

（兩位 sales 看到僵局，從店中出來，熱情招呼。）

Sales 武　　人逢喜事精神爽——

Sales 莉　　四季溫柔拍婚紗！

Sales 武　　來，大家請進，請坐。

Sales 莉　　要不要來杯法國紅石榴冰茶？（四人皆無回應）

裴裴　　　　這是 Tony ，這是小周，這是我媽媽。我和他們兩

　　　　　　個都來「二十一世紀台北尖端婚紗攝影」拍了天長

　　　　　　地久系列，就是這麼回事。我做了什麼天地不容的

　　　　　　壞事嗎？我很「惡劣」嗎？（故意學著流行的手

　　　　　　勢。）

三人一起　　沒有！

裴裴　　　　你們為什麼這樣瞪著我？

小周　　　　我沒有！裴裴。

Tony	我沒有！裴裴。
錦華	我也沒有！裴裴。（過去拉裴裴到身邊）來，裴裴，媽有話跟妳說，妳看著我。
Tony	裴裴，妳看著我！
小周	裴裴，妳看著我！
裴裴	你們都不了解我。（看著他們，甜美而又無奈的）其實我……（拍拍他們，親親媽媽……離去。）
錦華	裴裴，妳回來……

（眼看女兒不理她，又看到小周和 Tony 站在一起的尷尬景象，很不開心的逕自搬了一張椅子坐下。）

（小周也拉了一張椅子坐在準丈母娘的附近，Tony 本想離去，但是又決定走進店中，坐在另一邊。）

（音樂也尷尬的響起，sales 武和 sales 莉端著高腳杯冰紅茶，送上來給他們飲用，三人各有不同的反應，燈漸暗。）

第四景

（二樓平台漸亮，搖椅上坐著外婆君美，她身旁地上坐著繽繽。祖孫二人在落地檯燈下，翻閱著雜誌，繽繽抬起頭，充滿知性的問阿媽）

繽繽　　　　外婆，在這個世界上，妳還想去什麼地方旅行？

外婆君美　　不知道還想去什麼地方呀。埃及尼羅河……、長白山……

繽繽　　　　真的？爲什麼想去那裡？

外婆君美　　美國、加拿大、夏威夷去過了，歐洲也有旅遊二十一天過了。巴里島也有去過，上次跟はるこ阿婆的農會去過，也不錯。

繽繽　　　　埃及有金字塔。

外婆君美　　很古老、很神秘。也想去看古老的森林。聽起來，埃及離非洲近不近？

繽繽　　　　近，就在北非。唉，阿媽，妳都不會怕？

外婆君美　　去遊玩當然不會怕，就是想去看看那些跟台灣不一樣的地方。妳問這個做什麼？妳呢？

繽繽　　　　我想去人更少的地方，不知道咧，月球好了。
　　　　　　外婆，日本呢？妳怎麼不去日本？

外婆君美	還沒有去日本喔，奇怪，不知道為什麼還沒有去。很近咧日本。我日本話還可以講。
	以前我好想去啊！年輕的時候，聽到別人從日本回來，都心裡怦怦跳。大概是很羨慕吧，現在不去就算了，去看看也好啦，無所謂啦！
繽繽	我以為妳很想去日本，我也想去日本。
外婆君美	妳喔！妳想去月球就快點把錢存起來，買太空票。啊不，做太空人好了，做太空人要鍛鍊身體。
	妳每天晚上有沒有讀書？用功？還是在看小說？有沒有玩電動？
	妳說妳上國中之後不要再玩電動！
繽繽	（被阿媽講的有點難以招架）我很擔心讀下去的都會忘光光，我們的腦細胞每年都會減少，每天都會減少十萬個、二十萬個。
外婆君美	（站起來）妳這麼小還怕忘光光，我們做老阿媽都不怕忘光光，每天看報紙、看書，一直看一直看，怕什麼忘光光。
	（又回過頭來問繽繽）妳說的那個腦細胞每天減少十萬、二十萬？敢有影？怪不得罵人「空空」，就是頭殼裡面空空。

（此時繽繽突然感應到裴裴在樓下，徘徊走動。）

繽繽	姊姊在下面，裴裴！姊姊！（裴裴不語，悶悶地在左舞台的花台、路燈間，環來繞去。）
	荷花　荷花　幾月開
裴裴	一月不開　二月開
繽繽	荷花　荷花　幾月開
裴裴	二月不開　三月開
繽繽	裴裴！姊！
裴裴	（開始往繽繽的方向走去）荷花　荷花　幾月開　三月不開　四月開（從舞台後的隱形梯子上二樓）
繽繽	荷花　荷花　幾月開
裴裴	（聽到她的聲音）四月不開
繽繽	五月也不開
裴裴	六月也不開　七月也不開
	（見到裴裴已走到平台）
	荷花　荷花　幾月開
繽繽	八月開　九月開　十一月開？　十二月開？
裴裴	我本來想，明年一月開。
繽繽	一月開了就好過年了。
裴裴	（不理會妹妹，投入阿媽懷中）阿媽，我完蛋了。
外婆君美	怎麼會完蛋？荷花荷花怎麼會完蛋？裴裴，（把圍巾給裴裴披好）如果妳是煩惱和妳媽媽要挑的不一樣，那就先給它拖一拖，（台語）荷花較慢開不要

緊。

裴裴　　　　（靠著外婆，妹妹也黏過來）這下有得拖了。阿媽、
　　　　　　繽，我能不能告訴妳們？

外婆君美　　妳到底要哪一個丈夫？

繽繽　　　　我看妳兩個都愛。

裴裴　　　　（點點頭，慢慢站起來）我覺得一個女人一生只愛一
　　　　　　個男人是不可能的，嫁一個丈夫不夠，我要嫁兩個
　　　　　　丈夫。

繽繽　　　　（大樂，在後面轉圈）荷花　荷花　幾月開　荷花
　　　　　　荷花　幾月開

外婆君美　　（也站起來，正色地）裴裴，這個想法，真是……太
　　　　　　……真是太……這要怎麼說……真是……「帥呆
　　　　　　了」！

繽繽　　　　妳去跟媽咪講實話，媽咪說不定心裡面完全贊同。
　　　　　　我常常在想媽媽為什麼都沒有外遇？她那麼浪漫，
　　　　　　每天精力無限，那麼漂亮，好像天天都在跟誰談戀
　　　　　　愛。
　　　　　　跟爸爸講好了，爸爸比媽媽更願意放下身段。他說
　　　　　　不定更了解，如果家裡可以多一個男生，他也不用
　　　　　　那麼累。

外婆君美　　裴裴，說出來比較沒關係。

裴裴　　　　可是媽媽現在在婚紗店裡生氣，我……

外婆君美	直接走下去，直接走進去，把妳剛才講的，用比較好聽的話告訴他們，就好了。
裴裴	（一語雙關）從這裡走下去嗎？
繽繽	這樣比較快！
外婆君美	對！（裴裴受到鼓勵，往婚紗店樓下下去）
繽繽	哇！酷！我要去告訴我的同學，瑞琪還有世文。 （跑出去，從後面梯子下）
外婆君美	（獨自站在椅子前）我想，我嗎？我要好好想一想，再去告訴我的那些──「同學」。

（二樓燈暗。）

第五景

（婚紗店內燈亮，裴裴出現在三位枯坐的人面前。）

裴裴　　　媽，我來好好解釋一下，我要怎麼結這個婚。
　　　　　（走向小周）上大學的時候就認識你，三、四年來，
　　　　　你一直使我很快樂，你教我好多東西，你讓我覺得
　　　　　有依靠、有方向，我的同學都好羨慕。（摟著他的
　　　　　肩膀）你又這麼帥，我真的喜歡跟你在一起，你從
　　　　　來不讓我感到孤單。

小周　　　Love you，裴。

裴裴　　　（裴裴親吻小周的額頭，再走向 Tony，牽起他的手，繞
　　　　　著他的椅子，浪漫的拉起自己的裙擺）
　　　　　是你走進我的生命，讓我完成另一種狂放的喜悅，
　　　　　讓我看到海水的顏色和海洋的深沉。認識你才七、
　　　　　八個月，但是已經有一輩子的感覺，我愛你。
　　　　　（小周聞言站起，媽媽錦華也吃驚的往前走，但裴裴仍
　　　　　大方的對小周說）
　　　　　我也愛你。

錦華　　　沒有想到我的女兒會說出這種話。

裴裴	你們都要求我嫁給你們。現在讓我來向你們兩個求婚，少了你們之中的任何一個，我都有缺憾。 做我的新郎，請兩位做我的新郎，做我的「複製新郎」吧！（兩位男子並無回應） 媽！我也想過想學你的樣子，只是我做不來，而且，做你，太累了，我想誰都不必那麼累，Tony 你不必像小周，小周，你更不必學 Tony。（她牽著他們，誠摯的表達讚美和愛意。）我心中又想安穩，又要任性，又要溫柔，又要反叛。和你們兩個在一起，就此生無憾。以前我們可以這樣發展……現在，難道不能一起相處，一起結婚？
Sales 莉	一個新娘、兩位新郎的婚禮。
Tony	裴裴，妳真是青出於藍。
小周	裴裴，我真的把妳寵壞了。
錦華	同時「娶」兩個丈夫，還是「嫁」兩個丈夫？我真不相信我的耳朵。
裴裴	可以嗎？
Tony	No, no, 裴裴。
小周	No, no, no, no, 裴裴。
Sales 武	這個想法其實還不錯，我們倒是可以配合。
小周	這種婚禮還是免了吧。
Tony	連這種同居方式，我都不見得受得了。

小周	我也不要跟你這種人住在一起！
Sales 莉	不要急、不要急，我想這個婚禮的事可以以後決定，我們……怎麼樣？先拍一張王子和公主和王子的婚紗照試試看吧！
Sales 武	看看感覺怎麼樣再說！

（小周和 Tony 同聲嘆氣。）

Sales 莉	衣服嗎……要不要試試看同一款式的銀白鑲藍邊的小禮服……
小周	瘋了。
Tony	瘋了。（與小周同聲）
Tony	裴裴，妳的點子太厲害，要我這樣做，目前我是做不到。
裴裴	媽，妳聽見了，是小周不肯跟我結婚，不是我。而且，現在連妳看不順眼的 Tony 也不肯了。
錦華	（還是想把裴裴拉到一旁）裴裴我還是想跟你談一下。
裴裴	我才要跟這兩位好好的談一下呢。
	（對他們倆都伸出手，小周不得已跟著，為難的說）
小周	裴裴，妳又要說服我了，不過兩個丈夫是不可能的……。

Tony　　　　到了二十一世紀，人類經歷鉅變，說不定會比較謙

虛，喂，（對婚紗店宣告）花點時間和技術說服我們

吧，有一天，我們說不定會答應。

（一轉身，撞見錦華，收起狂放的態度，禮貌的對她鞠

躬）伯母。

（二位男友若即若離的跟著裴裴，熱烈發言，走走停停，經過巷道時，

觀眾仍看到這二男一女，彼此變化著關係與身姿，然後消失在右上

角。）

第六景

(婚紗店接待處只剩母親錦華一人，她的丈夫從舞台左側趕上來，瞥見三人離去的背影。)

丈夫　　都弄好了？他們上哪去？我來晚了？停車位太難找了，你不是在等我付帳吧？

錦華　　（有點好笑）不是，女兒大概婚結不成了。

丈夫　　他們不是一起走的……怎麼回事？

錦華　　（去坐下）裴裴在小周面前說──

丈夫　　（也跟著坐下）要跟那個 Tony ──

錦華　　那還好，他說要跟 Tony，還有要跟小周。

丈夫　　喔？他們兩個怎麼說？

錦華　　還怎麼說，當然不肯。

丈夫　　所以女兒長大了……

錦華　　沒想到長這麼大了。

丈夫　　那現在……（對 sales）這個錢要怎麼算，我們結個帳。（對錦華）先回家再說吧。

阿浩　　他們已經拍的部分不多，但是禮服已經在設計了，布料是進口的，而且這個訂單是有違約金的。最好

	還是拍一拍。
錦華	沒有婚禮還拍什麼？
Sales 莉	沒有婚禮當然更可以拍了。譬如 月下花前系列、山盟海誓系列，都不需要婚禮。還有情人節大餐專案、全家福慶生會和週年紀念。
	對了，你們何不拍一組結婚週年紀念呢？
錦華	（抬頭看丈夫）他才不會肯。
丈夫	老夫老妻了，拍這個幹什麼。
錦華	我就知道你會這麼說，我當然老了，老太婆了。
眾 Sales	（你一言，我一句，強力說服）
	年輕！
	有沒有四十歲？
	看起來和裴裴小姐像姊妹。
	那有這麼年輕的丈母娘？
	先生你說是不是？
丈夫	請你們，（伸出手擋一擋）請你們，讓我和我的太太自己說話好不好？真的，後退後退。

（眾 sales 也不太好意思，一步一步退後。留他們兩個自己坐在接待處的明式椅上談話，燈光漸轉為暈黃柔和。）

| 丈夫 | （轉向錦華）妳老太婆了，那我怎麼辦？那我不是更 |

老？（做誇張的動作）看不見了……牙齒掉了……肚子大了……

（錦華破涕而笑）妳真的掉眼淚了？為了裴裴？裴裴語出驚人，裴裴就是喜歡在我們面前語不驚人誓不休，這妳也不意外嘛！其實也蠻像妳的，女兒從小都學妳講話。

錦華　我講話不會這樣，不顧到別人的感覺，我講話都是有內容的。

丈夫　她這次倒蠻有內容的喔，她是真的這樣想嗎？一個女的，兩個男的……

錦華　我不知道，我只知道她跟小周很要好，又跟 Tony 瘋在一起。平常交兩個男朋友還可以……可是，這……（看看婚紗店，嘆息）

丈夫　其實很多女人有兩個男人……也有很多男人有兩個女人……

錦華　你這話是什麼意思？

丈夫　到底是愛兩個比較幸福，還是愛一個比較幸福，這倒不一定。

我自己是覺得也許兩個比較幸福，可是愛一個比較幸運。幸福要付出代價去追求的，幸運可就是從天上掉下來的了。

老太婆，妳就是從天上掉下來的。　（錦華依過去）

追求幸福不但要付出代價，而且可能還會很頭痛。裴裴是個聰明的女孩，她也許不怕頭痛，那個 Tony 好像也是天不怕地不怕，嘿嘿，他本身就是個大頭痛，妳一想到他頭就痛。

小周跟我這種人差不多，很平和，其實什麼事都能 handle。沒問題的，年輕人的事讓他們自己去 work out，我們不管了。

錦華　　管也管不了。

丈夫　　我們的女兒跟別人比，比是不必要的啦，不過也真的夠好了，她們沒有不良的毛病，沒有什麼不安，也不冷漠，都很積極，很 positive，又自信，也信任別人，裴裴和繽繽都是。我沒可挑剔的，她們也都還會長大，妳是比我操心……

（拍拍她的肩膀，摟著她，錦華也安適地對丈夫微笑。）

錦華　　你今天說的話好像比一個禮拜說的還多。

丈夫　　我把下個月的話也都說完了。

　　　　怎麼，心裡好過點了嗎？

錦華　　我生裴裴的氣，也是爲了她，也是氣她把我當成不能溝通的老媽。聽你的，操心也沒用。

　　　　大概我也有點失望吧！本來想做個風光丈母娘，女兒結婚，跟著興奮。我們結婚的時候，孤孤單單的，家裡一個人也不在身邊。

只有教授、朋友來教堂觀禮，在草地上開茶會。相片也是你 roommate 拍的，每張都歪的，還把我都拍出格了。

丈夫　　拍照……假如妳再來一次的話？我現在不是說拍照，我是說結婚這椿事，就這件事本身，妳，現在的妳已經很不一樣了，妳還會嫁我這個老土？這款草地郎，不會講話，又難看。

錦華　　你那時候比現在更土，擱較草地，不過你老了，好像還好看一點，只是更笨了，妳眞的不知道我一直都在跟你談戀愛。

丈夫　　一直都在做我的新娘，知道，故意問的。

錦華　　而且你老了更「惡劣」。

丈夫　　（回頭）好，我們自己拍一張，

（早已伏伺在四方的 sales 和攝影師、造型師，一湧而上，拉起他就往後面走，錦華和丈夫掙脫不了，但努力發言。）

丈夫　　先講好，那種怪里怪氣的衣服我不穿。

眾 Sales　不會怪里怪氣，不會——

丈夫　　拍一張正常的就好。

眾 Sales　正常——，正常——

丈夫　　普通一點的……

（他的聲音完全被淹沒，錦華跟著 sales 莉也往後面去更衣。）

眾 Sales　　普通，很普通。

Sales 莉　　我們可以把你們的皺紋都修掉。

丈夫　　　　（在後面不知為何突然地大叫）不要不要不要……

（婚紗店燈漸暗。）

第七景

（舞台左後方的樹下，打出旋轉的樹影光波，音樂琤瑽。戀愛中的繽繽
站在那裡等人，瑞琪上來，兩人互相凝視。）

繽繽　　　我喜歡你的眼睛。

瑞琪　　　我喜歡你的眉毛。

（世文上來，看著兩個女孩子，他走到繽繽身邊，對她說。）

世文　　　我喜歡你的嘴唇。

繽繽　　　（繽繽走過去對著世文）我喜歡你的笑容。（然後轉身
　　　　　靠著他）

世文　　　（世文把手放在繽繽的肩上）我喜歡你的肩膀。

瑞琪　　　（走過去，抱著繽繽的腰，輕輕蹲下來）我喜歡你的
　　　　　腰。

世文　　　我喜歡你的手。

瑞琪　　　我喜歡你的右手。

繽繽　　　（對著瑞琪）我也喜歡你的手。

　　　　　（對世文）我也喜歡你的左手。

（三人依偎了一會兒，然後轉為整齊花稍的舞步往前走，到舞台前緣外立定，再輕鬆說話。）

繽繽	所以，真的可以把基因修正到自己喜歡的那樣嗎？
	可以複製一個更好的、更漂亮的，
瑞琪	更會做數學的。
世文	更會考試的、打電腦更快的。
瑞琪	更會說笑話的、更會演戲的。
繽繽	自己？
	不對不對，我們要採用的是胚胎複合的方法。
	（她鄭重的蹲下述說）
	一個培養盒是妳的卵子，一個培養盒是我的卵子。
世文	（他跪在地上，雙手向前張開）繽繽的，瑞琪的。
瑞琪	（也坐下來講述他們共同的計畫）然後把世文的精子注入繽繽的培養盒和瑞琪的培養盒，在黑暗中受精，幾天後再把兩個培養盒裡的胚胎挑出來。
世文	要胖胖的、可愛的。
繽繽	都很可愛。
	把繽繽盒裡的胚胎和瑞琪盒裡的輕輕推在一起，再放在培養盒裡多待幾小時。
瑞琪	就是結合繽繽、瑞琪，還有世文的新胚胎。
世文	生命的共同體。

（三人滿足的微笑。瑞琪往前推推世文的腿。）

瑞琪	世文，你說你要懷孕。
世文	今年九月已經有第一個三親 three parents 的 baby 誕生了。
繽繽	那和我們計畫的不一樣。
世文	對，我是說，有了桃莉羊，又有 "three parents"，那本書上說，我們現在計畫的三親可以在二○一○年實現。
瑞琪	一定會很快！
世文	對，而且懷孕的問題會解決，我懷，或是另外一種培養箱可以懷。
瑞琪	像「侏羅記」。
繽繽	不是啦，恐龍是卵生。
	（三人輕快地蹦跳著往婚紗店去）
	媽！爸！

（婚紗店內已架好攝影器材，花團錦簇中，母親錦華和父親一起穿著象牙白正式禮服，坐在雙人沙發上拍照。）

造型師 Andy	這是你的女兒？小妹，要不要一起拍？
繽繽	媽，妳還好吧？（摟摟媽媽）我不要拍。（去父母中

間坐，但對攝影師搖手。）

錦華	還是繽繽比較聽話，嗯——（親女兒）
丈夫	妳姊姊的事都跟妳講了？
繽繽	爸，我只要一個丈夫。（看爸爸，轉頭再看媽媽，再面朝前）可是我也要一個妻子。（父母吃驚互看，難掩奇怪的表情。） 我喜歡女生、也喜歡男生。男生和女生不一樣，我覺得都要在一起，生活才有意思。
丈夫	喜歡跟愛不同……
繽繽	那我就是愛。（站在一旁的世文和瑞琪，對她呼應、附和）
世文	繽，520，我愛你。
瑞琪	5120，我也愛你。
繽繽	5200，我愛妳你。

（三人同聲大喊：7799，長長久久。配上動作，母親錦華有點惱了）

錦華	繽，讓我們先拍吧！
繽繽	（跳下來和友伴勾在一起）我們會在二〇一〇年結婚，而且準備有一個我們三個人生的小孩。高中聯考之後，我們會先找尋一家有能力處理這個方案的醫院，把我們三個人的名字，列入預約的名單中，這件事我們都討論過很多次了。

丈夫	華，沒想到這個女兒更天才。
造型師 Andy	二○一○年結婚？如果兩位家長同意的話，要不要現在先下訂單，我們會為小小姐特別設計禮服。
Sales 婉	我幫妳算一算，到時候還有的賺咧！
錦華	（站起來，對婚紗店員的態度不滿）喂——
繽繽	不要緊張，我才不要來婚紗店。
瑞琪	我們自己會拍。（拿出相機，對婚紗店裡的人猛拍）
世文	（也做同樣的拍照動作）我們互相用數位相機拍下我們在一起最值得紀念的時刻，然後每年做成一張 VCD。
繽繽	我們不需要婚紗攝影。（三人又集合在一起）我們知道這世界不是絕對的好，我們也知道它有離別、有衰老。
世文	但生化科技在二○一○年就會轉變，這個衰老的問題……
瑞琪	是的，不過我們不用擔心，是還早啦！
繽繽	（一邊一個，牽著親愛的男友、女友，在舞台中央，真摯的說）然而我們相愛，一生只有一次的機會，請世代的新娘……
世文	（輕聲抗議）新郎呢？
繽繽	好，就說新郎新娘，嗯，新娘新郎，俯聽我的祈禱。

三人同聲	（唱出）請給我們一個長長的夏季。
繽繽	給我們一段無瑕的回憶。
世文	給我一顆溫柔的心。
瑞琪	給我一份潔白的戀情。
繽繽	（吟誦下面的詩句，另外兩個哼著上面的曲調）

我只能來這世上一次，

所以，請再給我一個，嗯，請再給我，

不只一個美麗的名字，

好讓他們能在夜裡呼喚我，

在我們早已成長的年輕歲月裡奔馳，

但還是永遠記得，我們在一起相愛的故事。

（他們對著相機，三人自己給自己拍了一張合照。）

一，二，三！嘢——

（歡呼後，三人奔跑由舞台左區下。）

經理 Jeff	我們可以拍了。
	阿浩，音樂準備。
造型師 Andy	音樂下，培養一下氣氛。

（浪漫旖旎的西洋老流行歌"The wedding"流出音響。）

經理 Jeff   放輕鬆，卡嚓。（眾人忙著換景）

造型師 Andy   下一張娘娘躺下，老爺坐著。

（錦華夫婦聞言照做，造型師 Andy 一回頭，才發現錦華躺在地上。）

造型師 Andy   我是說老爺坐在椅子上，娘娘躺在老爺懷裡。

Sales 婉   誤會，誤會。（幫他們調整姿勢）

經理 Jeff   這樣很好。

                 來，拍了。

造型師 Andy   下一張娘娘站在椅子上，像雙飛燕這樣子。（示範
給他們看）

                 腳抬高，腳抬高。

（錦華依言，手扶著丈夫肩膀，盡量舉腿作飛躍狀。）

（又走到丈夫這邊，要他也把腿向後舉起來。）

丈夫   我自己來，我自己來。

                 （還是被扳了一下）

丈夫   唉呦！

（錦華趕忙去救丈夫的腰。而 sales 們還是把他們扳回原來的姿勢，大拍
其照。接著錦華頭紗掉地上，阿浩匆忙間卻戴在丈夫頭上。）

造型師 Andy   這樣也還不錯。

	老爺，您就扮演娘娘的新娘；娘娘，您就扮演老爺
	的新郎。
	來，老爺，嘴巴嘟起來，嬌嬌的樣子；娘娘腳打
	開，雄赳赳，氣昂昂的。（女雄壯，男溫柔含情。）
經理 Jeff	好，這樣很好。
	來，拍一張。
造型師 Andy	怎麼樣？滿不滿意？
	（錦華苦笑、點頭）
丈夫	（驚恐萬分）滿意滿意。
造型師 Andy	要不要再試幾套禮服？
錦華	（站起來）我想這樣就可以了。
丈夫	（站起來）我們可不可以趕快把衣服換回來？
Sales 祥	當然可以，請到這邊來。
	（兩人匆匆趕下去換裝，幾乎走錯了方向。）
Sales 祥	請到這邊，這邊，這邊。

第八景

（錦華和丈夫離場後，婚紗店的眾人，邊收拾東西，邊閒聊。）

造型師 Andy　其實這家小小姐的點子其實還蠻有意思的。

阿浩　你是說把相片作成 VCD ？看他們拿相機的樣子，將來變成同行也說不定。

造型師 Andy　不會吧？你真的以為那麼多的人會開婚紗攝影啊？

Sales 祥　當然囉！連那種結過婚的都會回來拍照，今天我們拍了新娘媽媽，以後還有新娘婆婆。

Sales 婉　而且我跟你保證，她們過幾年又會再來拍一次，留住青春，抓住人生美麗的尾巴。

Sales 莉　而且有的人結了又離，離了又結，婚紗生意強強滾。（往雙人沙發一坐）在台北市每一小時就有一對結婚，每兩小時就有一人提出離婚，我們不愁「沒頭路吃」。

Sales 勳　對面又開了一家。

造型師 Andy　他們還推出了 6900 新加坡蜜月拍照三天兩夜。（也去坐下，其他的人也聚攏來或站或坐。）

Sales 婉　隔壁還有喜餅二十四份的贈品。

Sales 祥	街角那家還送小家庭家電用品，整組！
阿浩	連隔一條街的那家老店也推出了「抽轎車」的廣告，好大一條紅布條從三樓整片掛下來。
Sales 莉	抽轎車，還有抽鑽戒呢！
Sales 婉	這又怎麼樣，別的行業也都在抽轎車，洗衣粉也在抽、洗碗精也抽，連買牛仔褲都在抽轎車。
造型師 Andy	就是說嘛！想結婚的人還是在看婚紗攝影的專業 quality，我們不要被這些有的沒的搞得頭昏腦脹。
Sales 勳	Yes sir！別家都有花招，我們也該想一些新的文宣廣告詞。（往前走，大家注視著他。）
Sales 勳	「新娘不死，婚紗攝影不止」。
眾 Sales	不能說死！你第一天做啊！
Sales 勳	嗯，哦！不能說死。「新娘不減少，婚紗全年無休止」。
眾 Sales	不好！太囉嗦！太長了！
Sales 勳	嗯，「新娘不減少，婚紗不會倒」。
眾 Sales	不能說倒！烏鴉嘴。
Sales 勳	好，「新娘不老，婚紗無恥」。（眾 sales 噤住無語，對 sales 勳怒目而視。）
Sales 莉	（痛捶 sales 勳）你才無恥。
Sales 勳	不好不好，這句更爛。
造型師 Andy	你行不行啊？

Sales 勳　　　我腦袋生銹了。

（此時兩位穿著瀟灑入時的男子，走進店門口，他們互看了一眼，隨sales 走到後面換禮服，台上只剩下造型師 Andy 一人。）

造型師 Andy　廣告呀！噱頭呀！固然重要，不過，像這樣的婚紗攝影是我們開創的，別家才跟進，只是，真正能夠了解他們的情感、品味和體態的攝影師不多，有sense 的造型師更少，所以，單拍王子跟王子就夠我忙的了。

（造型師 Andy 得意的一笑，拿著梳子往後面輕快的走去。）

第九景

（錦華和丈夫換回原來的日常生活服裝正要離去，聽見奇特的音樂、聽見秀貞說話的聲音。）

（秀貞站在二樓平台，樓上彩光旋轉，她也出現唸著招牌上的字：「二十一、世紀、台北、尖端、婚紗攝影、禮服」。）

Sales 勳　　　　有。

　　　　　　　（秀貞漸往下走）

秀貞　　　　　你們剛才在說什麼「新娘不死」？

Sales 勳　　　　被妳聽見啦？

秀貞　　　　　「新娘不老」？還有什麼？

Sales 勳　　　　歹勢啦！我們在想廣告想不出來，妳是從那裡跑出來的？

秀貞　　　　　廣告？你們真的什麼樣的事都辦得到嗎？……婚紗店。

Sales 勳　　　　對，和婚禮有關的事是我們的專業。在台北想結婚，跑一趟中山北路是少不了的，走進我們這家百年老店就更如魚得水了。

秀貞　　　　　百年老店？（笑）河裡有魚……

那你們能夠重新舉行一場我的婚禮，讓我這個（無聲地）「不老」、「不死」的新娘如願以償嗎？

造型師 Andy　（提高嗓門，讓後面聽見）古老的婚禮？你們記不記得？

經理 Jeff　當然記得！

Sales 祥　沒問題！

（經理 Jeff and sales 祥進來，在造型師 Andy 的主導下，他們幫著安排，為這「古老的新娘」裝扮著。觀眾也逐漸認出，他們三個也是上半場第五景中秀貞的父、夫、喜婆。其他的 sales 也即刻上場。
此時錦華和丈夫已走到門口，往舞台右側正要離去）

錦華　有人在說話的聲音像媽年輕的時候？不對，好像比媽媽還古老。阿母的阿母的款？那種味道。

（她還回頭往店裡望了一眼，但還是挽著丈夫由右側走出去了。）
（店裡面進行得熱鬧：「喜婆」準備把紅蓋頭給秀貞蓋上，秀貞卻主動地用手接過來。）

秀貞　我自己來。
　　　（她對著鏡子略為打扮，還刷了一下睫毛，把紅蓋頭拿起來比了比，放在一邊，卻拿起另一塊現代的白色婚

紗，自行披戴在頭上。秀貞走到扮演他丈夫的經理 Jeff

身旁，兩人並肩走了兩步，秀貞住腳，揭起自己的婚

紗，對造型師 Andy 反應）

我不要這個人，可不可以把他退回去。

（轉臉對 Jeff）

我不要你，退貨。

造型師 Andy　　沒問題。不過換人……，比較麻煩……

（以手勢示意，秀貞從寬袖中拿出個小紅包，交在造型師 Andy 手裡。）

秀貞　　　　　這樣擺平了吧！

經理 Jeff　　　那妳要嫁給誰？

秀貞　　　　　這不用你管，我自己找。

造型師 Andy　　好。讓妳自己選新郎。

（示意大家站好；所有男性的攝影師、 sales 、助理等，分布店中各個角

落，每人都擺出個特異的姿勢。秀貞穿梭來去，打量他們每一個人，然

後依照每個男生的模樣，講出她的評量，如：）

秀貞　　　　　太高——、太瘦——、太怪——、太凶——、太滑

　　　　　　　稽了——

（沒選上的男子們，也就一一應聲而旋轉下去。只剩秀貞。）

秀貞　　　你們這裡，只有這些人嗎？

（她走出店外，試著往台前那一片茫茫人潮望出去）

那裡還有人嗎？

（什麼也看不見，有點失望）

百年老店……

等了那麼久，讓我再當一次眞正的新娘吧！我想了
這麼久，讓我做他的新娘吧！

（她似乎想起了更多）

他，他……他……

他一定還會在那棵樹底下等我，他一定會的。

（臉上充滿著光輝）

我來了耶！喲……！我來了耶！你的新娘子眞的來
了。（她開始旋轉，對著台下，四方呼喊）你別躲起
來，你別不相信我……

（她記得了——，輕輕哼唱出）

一，二，三，四，五，六，七——

（更大聲了一點，帶著詢問，帶著搜尋）

一，二，三，四，五，六，七？

（徘徊、等待，不知要不要再唱）

情郎　　　（在觀眾席最遠方）

一，二，三，四，五，六，七——

（開始往舞台方向奔跑）

我的朋友在哪裡？在這裡，在這裡，（跳上舞台）

我的朋友在這裡。

（牽住秀貞的手，兩人旋轉，相擁，深情地互望。）

造型師 Andy　（跳躍到他倆身邊，故意輕輕喉嚨）

Well, excuse me!

（指揮大家，進行「古老的婚禮」）

一拜天地。

（秀貞與情郎轉身向外，虔誠鞠躬）

二拜高堂。

（兩人轉身向內正要鞠躬，男 sales 們興奮頑皮地擠上接待處正中的明式椅，接受他們的行禮）

夫妻交拜，送入洞房囉。

（兩人相對行禮，情郎揭起秀貞的頭紗，兩人微笑，溫柔相吻。）

（音樂大作，竟是西洋管弦樂演奏的「結婚進行曲」。他們挽著手翩然起舞。男 sales 們也都穿著黑色勁裝，在他們周圍灑著繽紛花雨，穿梭飛舞。

音樂再又一變，果然是強烈現代節奏的動感舞曲，全體 sales 由各方快速跳出加入競舞，氣氛熱烈而歡愉。舞蹈發展到後段，劇中所有的家族親友、情侶賓客也都上台，踩著自己的舞步，為常新的婚禮，不老的新娘慶賀。

而繽繽三小在階梯各處，蹤跳上下，外婆君美和錦華夫婦在二樓，也按拍舉手投足。裴裴牽著小周也挽著 Tony 出現，三人同步，在舞台較前方，也舞出交叉旋轉等花樣；偶爾小周和 Tony 突然捉對兒相舞，他們就不自然的跳開，然後回到裴裴身邊，再一回合後，兩個男子又舞在一起，裴裴微笑地和他們接掌穿梭，節奏越來越快……眾人越跳越激烈……)

（幕落。）

THE BRIDE AND HER DOUBLE
By Chi-Mei Wang
English Translation by Chi-Mei Wang

and Jeannie M. Woods

The Bride and Her Double

The Godot Theatre Company

Premiered at Taipei Novel Hall,Sep.11 1998

Original Play Written by Chi-Mei Wang

Produced by James Chi-Ming Liang

Directed by Chi-Mei Wang

Set Designed by Keh-Hua Lin

Lighting Designed by Tsan-Tao Chang

Costume Designed by Yu-Fen Tsai

Choreography by Hsiao-Mei Ho

Music Designed by Berson Wang

Stage Manager Chung-Yi Chi

Assistants to the Director Ching-Ting Yang, Lee-Ming Wang

Warm-up Master Yang-Yeh Fu

Cast

Fang-Shin Yen, Ying-Ju Tsai, Yu-Ping Lan, An-Die Chin, Yang-Yeh Fu, Su-Feng Chiu, Pi-Shan Chang, Yu-Lin Huang, Ya-Chen Su, Yung-Ching Wang, Chi-Hsun Li, Hsiang-Chih Wang, Wei-Chen Yu, Wu-Cheng Li, Wan-Ju Yeh, Li-Ching chang, Shin-Chih Jong, Pon-Cheng Hung, Kai-Ting Chiu, Hsiang-Chwen Chen, Hau-Kung Huang, Chi-Wan Chen, Chio-Ting Hung, Fu-Chin Chiang, I-Ching Hsieh

Setting

The action mainly takes place in the *21st Century Taipei Tiptop Bridal Photo Shop*. The stage is divided into the outer reception area (stage left), where we find two Ming-style chairs and lavish flower arrangements, and the inner salon (stage right), which has a platform with a parquet floor where the clerks can stage the photography sessions. On the walls of the shop are several sample gowns. There are several doors or passages leading to other rooms of the shop. There is also a mirrored folding screen upstage behind which clients can change clothes.

There is a staircase leading from the inner salon up to an upper level that is another dressing area of the shop. This upper level also has a rack of gowns at the back. At the up left corner of the reception area an opening leads onto the street, which runs along the back of the shop. The street can be seen through the upstage walls of the shop, so that the procession in the first scene can be viewed as it goes down the street.

Some areas of the stage double as a dining area, the room of Grandma Jun-Mei, the places where Bin-Bin meets her friends, a small plaza with several trees, etc.

The upstage wall behind the reception area is actually a wall with a matching panel in front of it. Both the wall and panel have two door-size portals in them. The panel can open up like a book flat, hinged on the stage right edge. In Act I scene 4, this panel is swung open and positioned so it runs from upstage (at the reception wall) to down right of center to create a facade to Hsio-Jen's house. The inner side of these panels is painted in a colorful abstract design that reminds one of a brilliant red sunset.

The Bride and Her Double

Principal Characters

Pei-Pei	A modern young woman from Taipei, about 25 years old; expecting to marry either Tony or Hsiao-Chou
Tony	Pei-Pei's boyfriend
Hsiao-Chou	Also Pei-Pei's boyfriend
Jin-Hua	Mother of Pei-Pei and Bin-Bin; a happily married career woman with a Ph.D. in biochemistry
Husband	to Jin-Hua; father of Pei-Pei and Bin-Bin
Jun-Mei	Mother to Jin-Hua
Hsio-Jen	A ghost from the past (Jun-Mei's mother, Jin-Hua's grandmother; great-grandmother to Pei-Pei and Bin-Bin)
Sweetheart	to Hsio-Jen
Bin-Bin	Pei-Pei's younger sister, about 14
Shih-Wen	Friend of Bin-Bin (male, about 14)
Rei-Chi	Friend of Bin-Bin (female, about 14)

Ensemble —The staff of the 21st Century Taipei Tiptop Bridal Photo Shop

Jeff	The manager of the shop and chief photographer
Andy	The hair and make-up stylist; he is gay–flamboyant and intensely energetic
A-Hao	The photographer's assistant (male)

Salesclerk #1 (female)   Salesclerk #5 (female)

Salesclerk #2 (male)   Salesclerk #6 (female)

Salesclerk #3 (female)   Salesclerk #7 (female)

Salesclerk #4 (male)   Photographer (male)

Minor Characters (also played by ensemble; doubled as shown)

Prologue

Bride (Salesclerk #6)

Groom (Photographer)

Relatives of the groom

I–5

Hsio-Jen's father (Andy)

Hsio-Jen's husband (Jeff)

Maids #1, #2, and #3

Wife #2

Matchmaker

I–7

Woman #1

Woman #2

Woman #3

Woman #4

Man #1

Man #2

Man #3

Man #4

I–8

Granny Plum

Principal

Husband to Jun-Mei

II–1

Old Man #1

Old Man #2

Old Man #3

Coach (can be doubled with actress playing Hsio-Jen)

Old Lady #1

Old Lady #2

Old Lady #3

Prologue
The Ritual of Leaving Home

As the curtain rises, the characters are caught in a freeze. The bride, in full wedding gown, stands in the center of the shop. The groom stands a few feet away from her. Around them stand three or four relatives of the groom. The staff from the bridal shop also surround them, holding various props: one holds up the traditional bamboo stick with a large piece of pork attached to its tip; one carries a large bamboo strainer, which will be used to cover the bride as she proceeds from the shop. The bride holds the traditional fan. Other people are arranging lights, positioning the cameras and light reflectors, and watching to make sure all the details are right. The very nervous groom holds the bride's bouquet of red roses. A cheery Taiwanese folk song is heard as the action begins.

Jeff	All right everybody? Places! Are we ready to go?
Andy	*(To the bride)* Oh, oh! Please don't cry! Tears will ruin our beautiful bride's make-up. *(He touches up her make-up a bit.)*
Sales 1	*(To the groom)* Oh, come on, now. No need to be nervous. *(To salesclerk 2)* Do something! He's starting to

sweat!

Salesclerk 2 mops the brow of the groom and fans him a bit.

Sales 1   Okay! It's time! It's time! This is the most auspicious hour. Let's give our bride a send-off she'll remember.

Jeff   Today is a wonderful day

For bringing two families together

Let's hurry and get on our way

Before there's a change in the weather!

(To A-Hao, the photographer's assistant) Come on, get ready for the shot.

(To the bride) You just stand here. Gracefully! Gracefully! Don't just stand there like a lamppost!

(To the groom) You don't have to worry about your pose. All eyes will be on the bride anyway! Just take the bouquet and hold it out to your beloved with a grand gesture.

The groom exaggerates this action, lunging forth and kneeling like a cavalier. Everyone laughs. The photographers snap the picture.

Andy	*(He holds their hands together as he speaks the verse)*
	One beautiful couple now sets forth to marry
	Two people facing both good times and bad,
	Three previous lives of good fortune they carry
	Four seasons of sweet peace are theirs to be had.
	(All applaud)
Andy	Good! Good!
Sales 2	Okay! Now everyone get ready. It's time for the bride to throw the fan, casting off all her girlish ways before she goes to her new home. *(To the staff)* Get ready to take the picture.

The bride exaggerates the action of throwing the fan. As she "winds up," the group follows her movement. She extends the fan in front of her, waist high, and sweeps it to the side, and then tosses it on the floor behind her. She breaks down in tears—she is happy, embarrassed, and sentimental all at the same time. The photographers capture the action in motion. One of the staff starts music playing—a happy Taiwanese folk song—which continues under the scene until the bride and groom are out of sight.

Andy	*(He scatters water from a bowl as he recites)*
	Water drops are scattered far and wide,

Like your love that showers him in joy;

True love lasts forever,

True love will ever abide.

(He repeats the verse as he continues the action.)

The group starts to leave the shop. They help the bride with her train, and follow her, one holding the bamboo strainer above her head, another carrying the bamboo pole to keep the evil spirits away.

Sales 2   Bride, groom, come right down the lane this way. Your car is waiting at the end of the street. We planned it that way so you can get right on the expressway. No danger of getting caught in a traffic jam right in the middle of the ceremony!

Ad lib from the staff: "Be careful." "Don't step on her skirt." "She's the most beautiful bride we've ever had." etc.

Jeff   *(Reciting)*

Heart to heart

A hundred-thousand years of good fortune and mirth,

Hand in hand

May your happiness last longer than sky or earth.

We see the relatives of the groom's family give a red envelope to Andy. The procession goes upstage and across the back of the stage, seen through the upstage walls of the shop. Jeff continues reciting as it goes.

The groom's so handsome and debonair,

The bride is delicate and oh, so fair!

Today you'll have a happy marriage,

Next year you'll wheel a baby carriage!

Congratulations! Congratulations!

The groom's so clever, so terribly smart,

He's certainly a very good catch.

The bride's so pure in mind and heart,

You're a perfect couple, a matchless match!

Congratulations! Congratulations!

He keeps repeating the verses throughout the procession. The salesclerks all stand and wave to the departing bridal party.

Andy　　　　*(Suddenly, he shouts a warning to them to be careful)*

Don't turn back![1]

All	Don't turn back! Never look back!

As the bridal party disappears, the sales people return to the shop and relax.

Jeff	Whew! We finally got them in the car!
Sales 1	I never dreamed this job would be so much work. I thought we'd never get done! No matter how long the bride stands there, I have to stand right by her. I tell you, my feet are killing me!
Sales 3	This leaving home ritual was just too much. It took so much time! In the future I don't think we should offer a discount for this elaborate a ceremony.
Andy	Yeah! First I had to get up early to put on her make-up and do her hair—that took four hours. And then I had to keep chattering all the time with his crazy old aunt! And everything had to be timed just right so it all came together at the exact, most auspicious time. It's too much!
Jeff	But some brides—like this one—don't have homes in

---

[1] Translator's note: It's considered bad luck to look back at this point.

Taipei. So our bridal shop serves as their parents' house and they begin the marriage ceremony right here in the shop. Don't forget that this little ritual is one of our best sales gimmicks. All the clever tricks we think up! We're famous in Taipei. And that's why we get so many well-paying clients. So I wouldn't complain too loudly!

(Beat)

Sales 1   *(Giggles and points to salesclerk #4)* And you—you are such a dope! We send you out for a pork chop to go on the bamboo pole. And what do you do? You come back with a package of shredded pork! *(Laughs.)*

Sales 4   Well, how did I know that the pork seller chopped up that pork? I didn't see it before he wrapped it up.

Andy   Where did you get the idea to go to the Ching Kuang Market to get the pork, anyway? It's just a good thing I opened the package to check.

Sales 4   Well, in my personal opinion, the pork from a good, old-fashioned street market just tastes better.

Sales 1   You idiot! That piece of pork wasn't for you to make into barbecue!

Sales 2   What did you open it for? Were you going to nibble on raw pork?

| Andy | All you guys should all thank me because I had the good sense to open up the package. Oh, well, enough about that. Our afternoon clients will be here soon. How many do we have? |

Sales 1   Hey, how much did she tip you?

Andy   *(Looking into the red envelope and smiling)* Well...it's okay.

Sales 1   *(With envy)* Such luck!

Sales 4   Now let's see. This afternoon we have Miss Pei-Pei. She's going to have the engagement photos—she's ordered the "Summer Love" package. She's already in the back, putting on her make-up.

Sales 5   I have another client at 8: 00. Her name sounds exactly like Pei-Pei. Would that be the same person? No, I guess not. This one wants the "Classic Beauty" package.

Jeff   Well, we'll find out soon enough.

(To Sales 1) Look at you: once you start gossiping you cheer right up and forget your feet are killing you. How about going inside and checking out the accessories for the photo shoot?

(To A-Hao) Prepare the lights! One "Summer Love" —coming right up.

The lights change and music comes up. Salesclerks 1, 2, and 3 leave the stage. Sales 5 enters.

Act I

Act I, Scene 1
Summer Love

Sales 5   Miss Pei-Pei! Please come out. We're ready for you now.

Tony and Pei-Pei emerge from behind the mirrored folding screen. She is a vivacious, charming young woman in a brightly-colored, romantic, flowing, full-length gown. Tony is handsome, easy-going, romantic and unpredictable. He wears a tuxedo that has a very loud black and gold-lame lining and matching cummerbund and tie. As they enter, the staff moves in a freestanding "Greek" column—a set piece for the photo shoot. Andy, the stylist, wheels in a cart overflowing with props, combs and brushes and ornaments for styling the hair, etc. Throughout the photo session Tony and Pei-Pei visibly enjoy each other's company; they laugh and tease one another and greatly enjoy the play-acting of the photo session. Pei-Pei is pinning a flower in her hair.

Pei-Pei   *(To Tony)* What do you think about this flower?

Tony   Looks kinda nice. *(Playing the director)* Act one, scene one, the beautiful Pei-Pei enters with flowers in her hair! *(They laugh together.)*

Jeff
All right! Come right over here. We'll get a shot right next to the Greek column. Just look at me right here. *(He motions for them to stand by the column and positions them there.)*

Andy
Oh, our princess looks just like a little Greek goddess! Just step back and then lean around the column. *(They follow his directions.)* Look right here!

Sales 5
Smile! Flash those pearly whites!

Jeff
Okay, great! *(He shoots several pictures)* Now, let's move to the next scene: Roman Holiday. *(The sales staff rolls in a large white fountain, and start to put Pei-Pei and Tony in place, dress their hair and touch up their make-up, etc.)*

Andy
(As Pei-Pei stands by the fountain.) Oh! Very nice, princess! Very pretty indeed. Come on smile! *(She beams.)* Ah! You look just like Audrey Hepburn! And you, Prince Charming, you just put your foot up on the fountain like this...

(He demonstrates a pose with one foot on the fountain, hand propped on knee.) That's it! You look just like Gregory Peck! *(Photos are shot repeatedly as poses are*

changed.)

Jeff	Okay! Look at her now. That's right, show her those great big brown eyes of yours. Now open up your jacket. *(He does so, to reveal the ornate lining.)* That's it! *(Photos are shot repeatedly as poses are changed.)*
Tony	Oh, wait a moment, please. I have a prop I want to use.

Sales 5 brings out a box with about half a dozen "wood roses" on long stems. This is a special flower that has the color of brown wood.

Pei-Pei	Oh, you remembered the wood roses!
Tony	Of course!
Pei-Pei	You know, the wood rose plant growing on my balcony doesn't have a single flower yet. It's nothing but a bunch of green leaves.
Tony	Don't worry. In the autumn those leaves will be gone and the flowers will cover the wall. Come on, let's get a shot with you holding the wood roses.
Andy	A very special flower for a very special lady!

Photos are shot repeatedly as poses are changed.

Jeff	Okay, look right here. Just relax and be natural. *(Takes pictures.)* Let's get one more shot with the flowers.
Pei-Pei	Okay, here...

She sticks the flowers in front of Tony's face, just as the camera flashes. All laugh.

Jeff	That's one you'll remember!

The staff repositions the set pieces. They move in a photographer's backdrop. This is a frame with several backdrops that can be changed by turning rollers at the top and bottom of the frame to create new backdrops. One might be a blue sky with white puffy clouds, another a garden drop, one a starry night, etc.

Tony	All these props give me an idea: maybe I should take a trip to Italy.
Pei-Pei	I thought you were going to Paris with me!
Tony	Ah, there are too many people going to France this year. So how about spending a year in Italy? We could travel for six months, then just enjoy ourselves, sketching, painting...

Pei-Pei   Oh, that sounds great! There's that interior design firm that wants me to go to work for them. A year in Italy would be a great opportunity to learn the trade. Oh! Florence, Venice, Milan...

Filled with the romance of the idea, she dances about as she names the cities of Italy. Suddenly she loses her balance and falls—rather gracefully—to the floor. The staff responds with adlibs: "Oh!" "Be careful!" "Are you All right?" etc. Tony runs to the embarrassed Pei-Pei and begins to help her to her feet, but is stopped by Andy's line.

Andy   Wait! Don't move! This is wonderful.

They shoot pictures. Tony then brings Pei-Pei halfway to a standing position when he is stopped again.

Andy   Oh, great! This is terrific. You can never get this kind of natural pose! (More photos are taken.)

Pei-Pei once more tries to stand upright. As she does so, she pulls on the skirt and innocently finds herself in the famous Marilyn Monroe pose from "Some Like It Hot." She is stopped with Andy's line.

Andy	Oh, my God! Marilyn Monroe! Hold that! *(They take pictures.)*
Jeff	That's it. Great! Another one! *(Many shots)* Okay, let's change to another scene.

Pei-Pei finally stands up fully. A-Hao goes to change the backdrop. Pei-Pei and Tony are moved to the side so the staff can set the scene.

Tony	I've been meaning to tell you that I entered a Public Art competition. They want artists to design an artwork for a park. When I saw the list of judges I knew they wanted some artwork that no one could understand. So I say "Great! Making incomprehensible art is my specialty!"
Pei-Pei	*(Affectionately)* Oh, really? I thought telling incomprehensible jokes was your specialty.
Tony	Well, if you laugh at my jokes, that's all I care about.
Jeff	Okay, over here now.

The staff steers them in front of the background—a starry night drop, perhaps with twinkle or tracer lights. They are directed to stand close together.

| Jeff | We're ready for the Shooting Star photos. Just look up here and pretend you see a shooting star. |

They look up as Andy and the staff adjust the dress, the hair, the body positions, etc.

Jeff	Now make a wish! *(They snap the picture.)*
	Now you see the shooting star, falling down this way. *(He gestures and they follow with their eyes as photos are taken.)*
	Now make your wish! *(They freeze, looking at the imaginary star.)* How about a wish for world peace?
Tony	*(Embracing Pei-Pei as the photos continue.)* I'd like to go see the park where they're going to put that artwork. It's in Taichung. Would you like to go with me?
Pei-Pei	When?
Tony	Well, we don't want to go on the weekend. There'll be way too many people. Why don't you take off a day or two from work next week. We'll go to Taichung, view the site, then spend the night in a little hotel I know in Puli.[2]

---

[2] Taichung is a medium-sized city in Taiwan on the western coast. Puli is a scenic little town further inland from Taichung.

As Pei-Pei and Tony continue to adjust their poses the photos continue. At this point, Pei-Pei kicks up one leg, with a bent knee, and Tony follows her action with his leg.

Jeff   Oh that's good! *(Takes photos.)* Now take another pose.

Tony and Pei-Pei both kick a leg front, in a knee-high high kick, ala Fred and Ginger. The staff adlib their approval: "Oh, wonderful!" "Hold that pose!" etc. Photos continue.

Andy   It's wonderful! Can you get those legs higher? *(They kick higher, laughing, as the photos continue.)*

Pei-Pei   *(Continuing their previous conversation.)* Oh, really? Just tell my boss I'm not coming into the office and skip off to spend the night in Puli with you? You are so romantic! Just like today—I had to call in sick to come do this photo session. You're really something!

Andy   *(To Jeff as he snaps the photo.)* I think that's about it, don't you? *(Jeff nods. To Pei-Pei.)* Miss Pei-Pei, are you satisfied? *(She looks at Tony, then smiles and nods to Andy.)*

Tony   Yeah, pretty good. I think it's okay.

Andy and Jeff motion for the staff to finish up. They clear away the props.
Tony and Pei-Pei begin to remove some accessories—the flowers in the
hair, the bow tie, etc., and move upstage.

Tony   Hey, do you want to go to @Live tonight? They have
              a great jazz trio playing.

Pei-Pei   Tonight? Oh, that may not be good. My mother wants
              me to get home early.

Tony   Oh, your mother is always like that.

As Pei-Pei describes her mother's routine, lights come up in a corner of the
stage representing her home. We see Jin-Hua, Pei-Pei's mother, laying a
cloth on the table, placing a bowl of fruit there, and then sitting back, put-
ting her feet up in a posture of great contentment and satisfaction.

Pei-Pei   Yes. Every night she gets off work, gets home to
              make dinner, then takes my little sister off to her
              piano or computer class. And then she'll come back to
              wait for Dad to get home so they can have dinner
              together. She'll want me there too.

Tony	All right, then I'm gonna get dressed and take off. You can take your time changing your dress and fixing your hair. So maybe we can go to @Live tomorrow night. Would you like that?
Pei-Pei	Oh that would be great. Tomorrow is ladies' night. So I don't have to pay!

They laugh and go off together upstage as the lights change to the next scene.

Act I, Scene 2
At Home with Jin-Hua

Lights fade in the bridal shop and come up in a small dining area in Jin-Hua's home. Her husband enters, removes his shoes and puts on slippers. Jin-Hua is an attractive woman in her late 40s or early 50s. She is a Ph.D. in biochemistry and enjoys both her career and family life. Her husband is the same age, a businessman of few words.

Jin-Hua	You're home!
Husband	Yes. I'm home.
Jin-Hua	Guess what we're having for dinner?
Husband	What are we having?
Jin-Hua	Your favorite soup: little silver fish with tender vegetables!
Husband	Mmmmmm...fish.
Jin-Hua	And rainbow bitter squash.
Husband	Mmmmmm...bitter squash.
Jin-Hua	And sauteed eel with miso sauce!
Husband	Who did you say got a skin peel?
Jin-Hua	No, no, no. I was just telling you what we're having

for dinner: sauteed eel with miso sauce! *(She gives him an affectionate little push or hit on the shoulder.)* Oh, you're sweating. Would you like to have a shower before dinner, or are you too hungry? Do you want to eat right away?

Husband   I've been starving since 4: 00 o'clock.

Jin-Hua   Oh, it's almost 8: 00! We'll eat as soon as the squash is done.

Husband   When the dogs went out this morning, Hwa Bau did his business but Ah Be didn't. I'll take them out for a walk before we go to bed.

Jin-Hua   We finally had that project meeting this morning. The coordination between the three labs is actually going to be very simple. We just have to work out the allocation of the funds. In comparison to our research projects, this is really a snap. *(Smiling)* I really don't know why these men make things so complicated!

Husband   Did you have a big fight with them?

Jin-Hua   No, you know I never fight with anyone. No, I just let them argue among themselves. Each one got his thirty minutes of glory and had his say. And the result is the very same it would have been if no one had spoken at all! It's difficult being the chairperson—all through this I'm laughing on the inside but on the outside I have to be really very serious, very concerned. How about your day? Were you busy?

Husband   Oh, today Peter had to dash off to Wuhan[3] and our boss arrived unexpectedly from Hong Kong to check on the new project. So this afternoon everything had to be done at once.

Jin-Hua   The contractor came out today and next week he will give us the estimate on building our new deck. When do you think we should tell him to start the job?

Husband   Well, why don't you decide that? Is Bin-Bin coming home soon? Is tonight her piano lesson or something else?

Jin-Hua   I think the materials for the deck are pretty good. Contractor Liu said it's better to use imported lumber.

Husband   I have to go out later, so I can pick up Bin-Bin. What about Pei-Pei? Where is she?

Jin-Hua   Oh, you have something to do tonight? I thought you were going with me to see Pei-Pei.

---

[3] In Mainland China.

Music comes up, as their voices fade and the lights slowly go down. Jin-Hua and her husband continue their conversation. We hear the last two lines clearly, then the rest of the conversation is "sotto voce."

Husband   *(With a smile, as if he didn't know)* Why? Where is she?

Jin-Hua   Surely you haven't forgotten—Pei-Pei's getting her photos taken at the bridal salon!

The husband takes out his paper. Jin-Hua gently extends her hand, to hold it down and keep him participating in the conversation.

Act I, Scene 3
Classic Beauty

As the lights fade in Jin-Hua's home, they come up in the bridal shop. Pei-Pei is discovered, wearing a very chic and elegant ivory bridal gown. Behind her is a hanging curtain of draped, gold fabric—perhaps with sheen like satin. The curtain drapes down on the floor and covers the platform to make a complete "set" for the photos. The shop staff moves around her, arranging the hair, the folds of the gown, her positions. Jeff is on the phone as the scene begins.

Jeff   *(Hanging up the phone.)* Princess! Mr. Chou said he'd
              be here right away.

Hsiao-Chou appears upstage, entering through the salon door, his cell phone still in hand.

Sales 6   Miss Pei-Pei, this style suits you so well. You can
              really carry off that casual, easy-going style, but you
              also look great in this sophisticated fashion.
              (She recites) Dressed to the nines

Or casual or breezy,

Your fabulous lines

Make my job very easy!

Hsiao-Chou enters.

Jeff	Oh, wow! Mr. Chou is here already. Please come in.
Hsiao-Chou	Hi, Pei-Pei! I hope you didn't have to wait too long for me?
Pei-Pei	It's All right. We just now finished with the make-up and hairstyle.
Andy	Well, Prince. That suit you have on looks great, but we still want you to go in there and try on another jacket, so you'll feel just right standing by your princess.
Jeff	You know, in taking your photos, it's not the clothes that matter. All our fashions look gorgeous. No. What's important is how the clothes make you feel— as if the costume matches your mood, your personality—when you put on the gown or the suit, you should feel magnificent!
Pei-Pei	How do I look?

Hsiao-Chou	You don't need to ask. Since we first drove by here I knew if you wore this dress, I knew you would look exquisite in this dress.
Sales 3	Okay now, let's take a pose. *(They strike a pose.)* Look over here.
Photographer	Smile! Open your mouth just a little bit more...
Sales 3	Oh, wait! Put a little powder on our Prince. (A-Hao powders Hsiao-Chou's face.) Such a good-looking couple! Your wedding is going to be just fabulous.

From this point on, the couple takes different poses and the staff arranges their hair, clothes and positions, and takes pictures.

A-Hao	Where are you planning to have the wedding? We can handle all the arrangements.
Pei-Pei	*(Speaking at the same time as Hsiao Chou)* Oh, it's still early.
Hsiao-Chou	Oh, it's pretty soon.

Pei-Pei and Hsiao Chou look at each other, the staff looks at them. Beat. Everyone laughs broadly.

Photographer	Oh, good. Keep laughing. Let's get a shot of that.
	(More photos.)
Hsiao-Chou	Someone is coming to see you later.
Pei-Pei	Oh, really? Who?

As Hsiao-Chou just smiles and does not answer, Pei-Pei keeps trying to guess.

Pei-Pei	A-Chang and Shiao Ling? Steve and his lover? Leu and his wife? Tell me! Who?
Hsiao-Chou	*(Smiling broadly)* "Her majesty!"
Pei-Pei	My mother?!! I don't believe it!
Hsiao-Chou	Believe it. She said she was coming. You'll see—she'll be so proud of you!
Pei-Pei	She said...you told her? *(Out of frustration, she lightly pounds him on his chest.)* Oh, I'm done for!
Hsiao-Chou	*(Humoring her, he sings)* "You are so beautiful..."

He turns her around and the staff captures the moment on film.

Photographer	Oh that's good! Smile! *(They shoot photos.)*
Pei-Pei	My mother! If she comes you know she will just...

Hsiao-Chou	If your mother has anything to say about the dresses, we'll just let her pick one out. Besides, when we came in here before you said she would like this ivory one.
Sales 3	Sometimes the mother's opinion is worth listening to. After all, the wedding is not just for the bride and groom. Many of your honored relatives will be there too.
Pei-Pei	*(Growing more petulant.)* If my mother knows all about this, then she'll expect me to get married very soon. *(Hitting Hsiao-Chou lightly.)* You! You'd better be careful! You can't go around just breaking the chain of command and giving reports directly to "Her Majesty." If you push me too much, maybe I'll decide I don't want to get married.
Hsiao-Chou	Oh, you don't mean that. *(He gives her a cuddle.)*

Sales staff ad lib: "Okay" "Let's get another shot" etc. As they take position, Hsiao-Chou spins Pei-Pei into a "dip" position, so she is held in his arms, her back arched and her head thrown back and her downstage arm holding the skirt. In this position, she catches sight of her mother entering through the reception area.

Hsiao-Chou	Bwo mu![4]
Pei-Pei	*(Appealing, like a little girl)* Mama![5]
Jin-Hua	*(Coming into the main room of the shop)* Oh, Pei-Pei. You look so very pretty! How many dresses have you tried on so far?
Pei-Pei	*(Trying to play down the importance of the photos.)* Oh, I'm just trying on one or two—nothing really...
Jin-Hua	Why don't you pick out some more? I think their styles here are kind of nice. Some are really special. Hsiao-Chou, don't you agree?
Hsiao-Chou	*(Aside to Jin-Hua, so the sales staff doesn't hear)* Yes, better quality than most and the price is quite reasonable.
Jin-Hua	Since you're already here, why don't you try on some more dresses? Let me see how you look in them?
Hsiao-Chou	Sure, you work so hard. It's not easy for you to get time off for this. Why don't you try on a few more? I could come back later, if you want.

---

[4] Translator's note: This is a Chinese term that has no equivalent in English. It is an honorary address for the mother of a friend.

[5] Mother is often referred to as "Ma" —the vowelsound somewhat more extended than in English. So that Pei-Pei's address sounds more like "Ma Maa" with the second syllable more accented than the first.

Sales 6	We have one dress that is just perfect for you. It's recommended by our fashion designer. It's brand new—would you like to try it?
Jin-Hua	Oh, what does it look like?
Sales 6	There's really nothing like it. The manager asked us to get that dress ready especially for Miss Pei-Pei. It's upstairs. When you see it, you will know what I mean.
Pei-Pei	Oh, really?
Sales 6	Well, it's up to you. Maybe you would like to experience this special, glamorous feeling?
Pei-Pei	All right.
Sales 6	Please come this way.

She gestures to the stairs going up to the other dressing room. Pei-Pei goes up, followed by Sales 6 and Jin-Hua.

Sales 6	*(To Jin-Hua)* We have many specially designed bridal gowns, but we don't display them in the window because we are afraid that people will take photos of them and copy our design.
Jin-Hua	Is that so? How can that happen? Doesn't the copyright law protect the designers work?

Sales 6	Oh, sure! When I see our beautiful designs made up in cheap imitations and sold on the street in the night market—well, I could just cry. *(They arrive upstairs.)*

As Hsiao-Chou changes back into his own jacket, he shakes hands with Jeff and leaves. Pei-Pei goes behind the rack of clothes at the back of the upper dressing room. During this scene, she will talk with Jin-Hua, poking her head through the rack of clothes as she does this. She has left her purse with Jin-Hua. After Hsiao-Chou exits, a beeper goes off in Pei-Pei's purse.

Pei-Pei	Ma! That's my beeper. It's in my bag. Would you please hand it to me? *(Jin-Hua does so. Pei-Pei gives a big smile when she sees the number of the caller—it is Tony.)* Ma! Please lend me your cell phone.
Jin-Hua	Oh, who do you want to call?
Pei-Pei	Ma! Don't ask! *(She tries the number, but it won't go through.)* The call's not going through. Maybe it won't work in this building?
Jin-Hua	*(Teasing)* You see, you don't tell me who you want to call, so my cell phone won't work for you. Hey...I thought *(small pause)* you two broke up already.
Pei-Pei	Oh, my dear mama. Who are you referring to? And

	what are you laughing at?
Jin-Hua	Me? I'm not laughing.
Pei-Pei	Let me tell you something. I will never break up with Tony!
Jin-Hua	Pei-Pei. I thought you were getting ready to be married!
Pei-Pei	I knew you would give me this kind of pressure...
Jin-Hua	I'm not pressuring you about anything. But what about all these photos? What is this all about?
Sales 6	After she takes all these beautiful photos, surely the wedding can't be far off.
Pei-Pei	Oh? I thought the staff of your shop said we could take some photos now and sign the contract later.
Jin-Hua	Come out and let me look at you.

Pei-Pei emerges from behind the rack, wearing a beautiful gown.

Jin-Hua	Wow! Pei-Pei, I think this one is extraordinary. *(Feeling the fabric)* These new fabrics feel and look so good.
Sales 6	This fabric is imported. It's very special embroidery— very elegant. The design was inspired by the movie, The Titanic.

Jin-Hua	If you decide on this one, then you can wear my pearls.
Pei-Pei	Oh, I think the lace is kind of nice, but I think pearls would just be so old-fashioned. *(To salesclerk 6)* Oh, miss, I think this one doesn't look good on me.
Sales 6	But it looks great to me! It's so elegant and it fits you so well. It sets off the shape of your face. And the cut over the shoulder is just perfect—so classic, so...
Pei-Pei	Too classic! Mother, this one looks more like your style. *(To salesclerk 6)* I'd like to try the one with the orange trim I saw downstairs.
Sales 6	All right, I'll get it ready for you. *(She exits to downstairs.)*
Jin-Hua	I still think this one is better.
Pei-Pei	Mother, you know what I'm thinking? I think you are like some aristocratic lady in the Taiwanese Opera who wants to pick out a rich husband for her daughter. This is all a romance...
Jin-Hua	What Taiwanese Opera? What romance are you talking about?
Pei-Pei	Ma, really. You always force me to make a choice!
Jin-Hua	Why do you say that? I was just happy to come here

	to see you and Hsiao-Chou take the bridal photos. I don't know what you're talking about. I only wish...
Pei-Pei	You wish me to pick a husband that will impress all our relatives.
Jin-Hua	No, I only wish you happiness. I just don't want you to commit yourself to a life of hardship.
Pei-Pei	What you want is for me to be just like you: to pick out an acceptable fiancé, to get married, have children, and be a housewife or—to be exactly like you, a superwoman! That I can't be and I won't be!
Jin-Hua	Ah, what are you talking about? Every day I work a little in the garden, I fix everyone breakfast, I work, and at night I turn out the lights and tuck everyone into bed. And my greatest joy is to go shopping for beautiful clothes with my daughter. What do you mean "superwoman" ? I'm just your average, everyday woman.
Pei-Pei	*(Removing a little cape or shawl from the dress and tossing it to her mother.)* You just don't understand what I'm trying to say. I'm going to talk with the shop designer. And please don't follow me! Please, "average, everyday woman," please go home. Don't wait

for me. Okay?

Pei-Pei goes down the stairs.

Jin-Hua   *(Left alone, she talks to herself.)* Actually, the only true
             wish I have for you is to marry someone you love.
             Just like me. "Just like me" sounds good. What's
             wrong with "just like me"?

*She starts to hang up clothes, then takes out a gown or two, looking at her
reflection in an unseen mirror.*

Act I, Scene 4
Jin-Hua's Memories

The lights come down to focus only on Jin-Hua; music in under dialogue.

Jin-Hua   To marry someone you love, to be a bride and walk
               down the red-carpeted aisle under the arbor of flow-
               ers, to hear the delicate strains of a string quartet play-
               ing, to get the blessings and good wishes from every-
               one on that special day, and to begin to write the
               beautiful poetry of your life together—isn't that what
               Pei-Pei has wanted since she was a small child? When
               she got to be the flower girl in the wedding?

               I never had a chance to be a flower girl. In those days
               few people had that kind of wedding. I gave Pei-Pei
               everything she ever wanted while she was growing
               up. When she was only four she was in her first wed-
               ding, carrying the bride's long train. Then at five she
               was the flower girl. In those days little girls liked to
               wear frilly little dresses and I made her a brand new
               one for the wedding. Whatever I didn't have, she was

always sure to have. When I was that age, five years old, we always wore hand-me-downs. I didn't get my first one-piece dress until I was in high school. And then I had to wait until my aunt could sew it for me.

When she was sixteen Pei-Pei was already inviting her friends to her birthday party at home. She was a good student then and very pretty. I remember that the young son from the Chen family liked Pei-Pei very much indeed. He had a round face and his hair was styled with a wave in the front, as though he was already working for a good corporation. *(Laughing)* But that night he was very disappointed and cried when he discovered that Pei-Pei didn't really like him at all. She was sweet on someone else! Not long ago someone told me that he had gotten married to the daughter of the President of Taiguang Corporation and he seems very happy and is doing well for himself. I wonder who told me that? Maybe it was Pei-Pei.

Now Pei-Pei is getting married before long. So why is she running so hot and cold, keeping things to herself? She's never been that way. When she was little she was so incredibly sweet, so close to my heart. Every day when she came home from school she would sit down and tell me everything that happened while I prepared supper. If I didn't respond to her, she'd get mad. And now, if I even ask a simple question, she gets angry. *(Pause)* Oh, heavens! I don't really understand what has happened to my daughters. What are they thinking?

Sales 1	*(Entering)* Oh, I didn't mean to disturb you. I just came up to look for something.
Jin-Hua	I'm sorry. I was just waiting for my daughter.
Sales 1	Is that the one who was changing clothes? Miss Pei-Pei? How fortunate for her to have a mother who cares so much for her. Is she your only child?
Jin-Hua	She has a younger sister. Much younger—she's just in Junior High School. In a way they are both an only child.
Sales 1	With such a difference in their ages, it must be difficult to look after them.
Jin-Hua	Well, when the younger one came it was easier because I could get help. I took care of Pei-Pei all by myself—with one hand I was feeding her and rocking

her cradle and with the other hand I was writing my doctoral dissertation. When I think about it today, I don't know how I did it. But I was young and I didn't mind getting tired. And I didn't know how hard it was! I was a full-time student, a part-time worker, and a full-time mom—all at the same time! And that's how I brought up Pei-Pei. The situation was better with the second daughter because we were back in Taiwan by then...

Sales 1   *(Pulls out a traditional, late 19th century Chinese-style wedding dress)* Oh, this one is in here!

Jin-Hua   You even carry the traditional Chinese bridal gowns?

Sales 1   It's our specialty to carry different styles and accessories for brides through the generations. You know, the photographer in this shop—his great-grandfather was also a photographer during the Manchu and Japanese periods. Many of the photos he took were of brides and his work is now displayed in the museum. We still have one of his photos downstairs.

As they talk we see a light come up on the photo in the shop downstairs.

Jin-Hua	My mother told me that my grandmother—that's her mother—wore this type of traditional gown. We used to have a photo of her at home, but it was lost during the August 7th flood. That was so long ago, I can't remember what she looked like. It's too bad I never knew my grandmother. She passed away when my own mother was quite young.
Sales 1	She must have been very beautiful because you and Miss Pei-Pei are so very attractive.
Jin-Hua	*(Demurring)* Hmmm... Well, thank you. We all inherited my mother's and my mother's mother's eyes.

As Jin-Hua thinks about what she has said, the Salesclerk steps closer and they continue their conversation softly as the lights fade out on them and come up to reveal Hsio-Jen, standing behind the photo. Music becomes otherworldly as we see this image of Jin-Hua's deceased grandmother as she looked when she was a young woman.

Act I, Scene 5
Hsio-Jen's Story

As the lights fade out on the upper platform, Hsio-Jen steps out from behind the screen and lights come up in the shop area. We are now in the past. Three of the salesgirls will portray Hsio-Jen's maids in this scene. The maids set the scene, bringing in an ornate "moon gate" screen and small stool and the Ming-style chair from the reception area. The maids wear the same black dresses they wore as shop staff, but they carry handkerchiefs and their gestures and body movements indicate they are from a time about 100 years ago.

Hsio-Jen takes a basket of embroidery and sits in the chair. This is her only possession. In it she may keep small trinkets, poems, letters. Most important is that here she keeps her "square characters." These are flat 2" squares of cardboard-red, with a single Chinese character on each one. Like children's ABC blocks, these characters are Hsio-Jen's education. At first she does a little embroidery on a handkerchief, but then she sets that aside and takes out her characters and begins to read. Each one has a different word on it.

Hsio-Jen	"Person." "Mouth." "Hand." "Knife." "Ruler." "Big." "Middle." "Small" . "Ice." ... "He."
Maid #1	*(Correcting her).* "Heat." *(Hsio-Jen looks at her, questioning.)* "Ice." "Heat" .
Hsio-Jen	Oh. "Heat." *(She continues.)* "1" "2" "3" "4" "5." "Up." "Down." "Heart." "Lord." Mmmmm... *(Unsure of this one, she shows it to the maid.)*
Maid #1	"Lady."
Hsio-Jen	*(Softly)* "Lady."
Maid #2	You know what a lady is? The lady is the wife, the bride.
Maid #3	You will be a bride soon.
Hsio-Jen	Me? No, I don't want to.

The three maids laugh.

Maid #3	You don't want to? That's not possible.
Maid #2	Your father already has made the decision. The arrangements are already made.
Hsio-Jen	But I want to read. I want to learn my characters. I want to... *(She holds back her last thought.)*
Maid #2	All right, if you want to learn your characters, why

don't you go ahead and read?

Hsio-Jen   *(She reads fast, serious, deliberately.)* "Person."
"Mouth." "Hand." "Knife." "Ruler." "Big."
"Middle." "Small" . "Ice." "He." "He..." "He..."
(she pauses.) "1" "2" "3" "4" "5." *(She slowly
looks at the window.)* "Up." "Down." "Heart."
"Lord." "Lady." *(She sighs, and turns back to her
basket.)*

*Hsio-Jen's childhood sweetheart runs onstage, happy and enthusiastic as
he echoes her counting. He takes large jumps, like hopscotch as he counts.*

Sweetheart   "1" "2" "3" "4" "5."

*He takes slow, big jumps on each number, moving closer to the door of
Hsio-Jen's house.*

Sweetheart   "1" "2" "3" "4" "5." *(He stretches out his hand to
her.)* "Ice."

*Hsio-Jen rises, jumps out the door and extends her hand to him as she
speaks.*

Hsio-Jen	"He!"

Together they sing a childhood song:

> One, two, three. Where can he be?
>
> Five, four, three. Can she see me?
>
> Six, seven, eight. Is he at my gate?
>
> Two, three, four. Here he is at my door!

Hsio-Jen	Up. *(She makes a gesture, extending her hand with the word.)*
Sweetheart	Down. *(He takes her hand and lowers it.)*
Both	Heart. *(They each gesture to their own heart with the word.)*
Hsio-Jen	Lord. *(She takes his hand and places it on her own heart.)*
Sweetheart	Lady. *(He takes her hand and place it on his heart.)*

At this point the scene becomes highly stylized in dance and pantomimic movement. In this way the story of Hsio-Jen's marriage is told. Romantic music under. She teases him, pretending to shoo him away with her scarf. This play evolves into a little dance where he pulls her to him, they turn together; when they both face front, he lifts her by wrapping his arms about her upper legs. He turns around with her in this lifted position, as she gently lays the pink scarf over her head, playing at being the bride. He puts her down and takes his long sash, putting one end of it in her hands. They move together, facing front and dancing to the left side of the stage. This is also a gesture of the marriage ceremony. He removes the scarf and adjusts the flower in her hair.

The romantic music becomes percussive and satiric as three figures appear up right, on a long diagonal opposite the lovers down left. The figures are Hsio-Jen's father, her fiancé, and the female matchmaker. They enter in a stylized movement representing a fast approach, running from a long distance away. After a while "running" up right, they move across the stage to the lovers. They pull Hsio-Jen backwards, towards the house at stage right. The matchmaker closes the gate of the house: this is done by swinging open the panel that was the back wall of the reception area. The wall swings into a position running from up center to down right of center. Its two portals now serve as doors to Hsio-Jen's house.

The father and matchmaker cover her head with a heavy red veil and push her to the new husband. The husband tries to lift the veil, but she holds it. They struggle and the scarf is pulled off. He shakes the scarf at her, teasing and exploiting her body. She pulls away from him, trying to turn away from

him, but he continues to torment her with the veil. She falls and he contin-
ues to harass her. She gets to her feet, trying to avoid his touch.

He tries to catch her with the scarf: he twists it into a rope and loops it
over her head and behind her waist, pulling her to him. She arches, back
helpless to resist. Finally, he sits in the ornate chair and, with her facing
him, he lifts her up before lowering her onto his lap. He shakes out the red
scarf, holding it up behind her so we cannot see her head and shoulders.
He ripples the cloth, to the accompaniment of the still raucous music. Then
he pulls the scarf up and onto her head. He wraps his arms around her
back and she arches back, so that her head touches the floor. The husband
mimes unbuttoning her clothes. Then he pulls her to him again. She stands,
making motions as if to button or pull her clothes together. He crumples up
the scarf and gives it to her. He relaxes in the chair, pleased with himself as
she dutifully mops his brow with the scarf.

The music becomes cheerful and Hsio-Jen slowly slips off right as the
matchmaker reappears stage left with the second wife. The husband sees
wife #2, he twirls the scarf into a sash and dances to the door to greet her.
Wife #2's stylized movement shows she is happy and flirtatious. When the
husband teases her with the scarf, she teases him back. He cheerfully
brings her into the house.

At this point, Hsio-Jen enters, visibly pregnant. Wife #2 bows to her. The husband is very pleased at Hsio-Jen's pregnancy and crosses to show his approval. Wife #2 grows angry and exits. She enters again, visibly pregnant, with a bigger tummy than Hsio-Jen's. When the husband doesn't respond, she grows jealous and bangs around the furniture to show her displeasure. The husband tries to calm her down. She grows happy and draws him back. As they exit upstage, Hsio-Jen sadly moves away, coming down stage.

Maid #1	Doesn't this bother you? If one day she gets the upper hand, what will you do? That would be intolerable! *(Hsio-Jen only shakes her head and gives a long sigh.)* In your heart you really don't like this. Otherwise, why do you sigh so?
Hsio-Jen	Oh, I'm just thinking of my own feelings.
Maid #1	What is in your heart? Why don't you tell us?
Hsio-Jen	You wouldn't understand.
Maid #1	Is there anything in a bride's heart that we can't comprehend? If we can't understand how you feel, who on earth can?
Hsio-Jen	*(Smiling)* I am only thinking about death. If I die, everything will be fine.

Maid #1	What? That's strange! Your bridal gown still shines and the buttons are brand new. Even the soles of your beautiful embroidered shoes are not yet dirty. And you still have delicate hairpins and pretty earrings you have not even worn yet. How can you even think about dying? Oh! Bad luck! *(Whispering)* Don't make things unpleasant for the household!
Hsio-Jen	But dying is pleasant. If I cannot be with him, I will be very unhappy in my heart.

Both maids draw back in astonishment. Feeling sorry for her, they leave her alone. Hsio-Jen takes her basket and goes out of the house. She sits on the edge of the platform, which represents the step outside her door. She slowly takes out the square characters and looks at them. Then, angry and hurt, she throws the characters, scattering them in the air as she calls out each one's name. She then collapses on the step.

Hsio-Jen	*(Crying)* Ice! He!

From the time that Hsio-Jen was taken away by the father, the sweetheart has slowly moved to deep upstage right, standing there, turned away, but still on the stage. Now he slowly moves towards her.

Sweetheart   On the other side of the mountain, there isn't any tree.

And on that mountain there isn't any bird. In that river

there are no fish. And in that river there is no water.

And the person on that side of the mountain has no

tears.

He crouches down, still at a distance from her.

Sweetheart   That person must be looking for me.

The Sweetheart begins to sing their song and Hsio-Jen slowly joins him,
singing and crying.

Both   One, two, three. Where can he be?

Five, four, three. Can she see me?

Six, seven, eight. Is he at my gate?

Two, three, four. Here he is at my door!

The lights change, to show that the lovers are meeting only in their imagi-
nation or dream. The sweetheart starts to walk to her. They repeat the
movements of their earlier game, but their moves are smaller and not so

joyous.

Hsio-Jen	Up. *(She makes a gesture with the word.)*
Sweetheart	Down. *(He makes a gesture with the word.)*
Hsio-Jen	Heart. *(She begins to make a gesture with the word.)*
Sweetheart	Heart. *(He takes her hand and pulls it to his own heart.)*
Hsio-Jen	Lord.
Sweetheart	Lady.

They embrace and caress one another.

Hsio-Jen	On the other side of the mountain there is a tree.
Sweetheart	This is the flower from your hair.
Hsio-Jen	You have been there, standing beneath that tree.
Sweetheart	When I picked up your flower, I knew I could never see you again.
Hsio-Jen	If I could just see you once more.
Sweetheart	If I could only see you again.
Hsio-Jen	Then my heart would not ache.
Sweetheart	Oh, please don't yearn for me. *(He changes to a happier tone.)* On the other side of the mountain, there is a tree. Yes, please don't be unhappy.

As they speak, they use simple, child–like gestures to illustrate their poetic thoughts.

Hsio-Jen	You are standing underneath that tree.
Sweetheart	There's a tree on that mountain
Hsio-Jen	There's a tree on that mountain.
Sweetheart	There's a fish in that river.
Hsio-Jen	There's a fish in that river.
Sweetheart	There's a bird in the tree.
Hsio-Jen	Birds in the tree. Feet under the tree.
Sweetheart	*(laughing)* Those are not feet under the tree!
Hsio-Jen	Then what is under the tree?
Sweetheart	There's a man under the tree.
Hsio-Jen	Yes! A man!
Sweetheart	There's a man under the tree. Someone is waiting for you.
Hsio-Jen	He is waiting for me!
Sweetheart	That's right. He is waiting for you. Fish are in the river.
Hsio-Jen	Yes, someone is waiting for you.
Both	Waiting for you. Waiting for you.

They move in a dance. It ends with her kneeling on one knee, her back to the sweetheart. One of her hands is held up, holding onto his hands. He slowly releases her grip and leaves. She does not see him go. She rises, looks about as if in a dream, then sadly walks back to her home. The lights fade out downstairs and come up again on Jin-Hua, still lost in her thoughts. Salesclerk 6 comes upstairs with a glass of juice, which he offers to Jin-Hua. During the remainder of the scene, the panel that made Hsio-Jen's house is folded back into place, restoring the reception area.

Jin-Hua	*(Continuing her recollection.)* My grandmother told my mother that if you get married, you should marry someone who is close to your heart. My mother also told me the same thing. I told Pei-Pei the same thing. But she never listens to me. No matter what I say, she hears just the opposite. But Bin-Bin will not be like that.
Sales 4	Is Bin-Bin Miss Pei-Pei's younger sister?
Jin-Hua	Bin-Bin is my little girl. Oh, I should probably give her a call.
Sales 4	I'll take this. *(He takes her glass.)*

Jin-Hua dials her cellular phone, but the call does not go through.

| Jin-Hua | My cell phone isn't working here. |
| Sales 4 | Why don't you use the downstairs phone? |

As they go downstairs, the lights fade out on them; Bin-Bin enters down left and lights come up there for the next scene.

Act I, Scene 6
Three's Company

In this scene, three locations are represented—one for each of the teenage friends. Each has a beeper upon which he/she will dial a code that translates into a personal message for the friend. Note that during this scene the Ming furniture from scene 6 is removed.

Bin-Bin   *(Reading the code on her beeper)* Five, three, zero. "I think of you." Oh, you've finished your homework and are thinking of me. Okay, I'll call you too.

She enters a code on her beeper and Rei-Chi's beeper sounds at the same time. Lights come up on Rei-Chi, down right. She reads the beeper code.

Rei-Chi   Five, three, zero. Oh, you are also thinking of me!

Bin-Bin   *(Responding to her beeper sounding and reading its message.)* "One, one, seven, seven, one, five, five, U." What is this? Let me see. One is "I." One seven seven is "M," one five five is "I, S, S" —MISS!

Rei-Chi   *(Speaking aloud the code she is entering.)* Seven, seven,

	nine, nine.
Bin-Bin	Right, I miss you! Oh, "One, one, seven, seven, one, five, five, U" means "I miss you!" *(Her beeper sounds again.)* "Seven, seven, nine, nine." "Long, long, ever, ever." Oh, this must be Rei-Chi again.
Shih-Wen	*(Lights come up on him at up center left; he puts in his code.)* "Zero, five, six, four, nine, three, three, five, eight."
Bin-Bin	*(Responding to her beeper and the long number.)* Oh, Shih-Wen always makes the longest codes! Let's see— zero, five, six, four means "When you feel bored," nine, three, three, five, eight means "then think, think of me." Oh, good, I'll call him. Shih-Wen, four, five. Oh, what shall I say? I know, "five, eight, four, five, two, zero." That should make him feel secure!
Shih-Wen	*(His beeper sounds and he reads the message)* "Five, eight, four, five, two, zero" means "I swear I love you!"

He gleefully jumps in the air.

Bin-Bin	*(Her telephone rings.)* Oh, the telephone! Who could

that be? Wei? Hello. Moshi moshi.[6]

Jin-Hua	Wei?
Bin-Bin	*(Surprised)* Oh, mother! It's you!
Jin-Hua	Wei? You're already home? Don't stay up too late, okay? Have you fed the cat yet?
Bin-Bin	I don't know where she is.
Jin-Hua	Well, if she doesn't want to eat, just leave her alone. You have a test tomorrow morning, so get to bed early.
Bin-Bin	But I still want to check my homework with my classmates.
Jin-Hua	There's some nice soup in the refrigerator. Have some if you get hungry. But don't eat too much ice cream! *(She hears Bin-Bin's beeper sound.)* What's that?
Bin-Bin	Oh, nothing, just my beeper.
Jin-Hua	Really? Is that Shih-Wen or Rei-Chi?
Bin-Bin	Both of them! I have to call them back. Bye-bye. *(She hangs up the phone.)*
Jin-Hua	Okay, bye. *(Hangs up the phone.)*

---

[6] "Wei," pronounced "Waaay?" is Chinese for hello. "Moshi, moshi" is Japanese for hello. (At this time in Taiwan Japanese music and customs are very popular with young-adults.)

All the three teenagers' beepers sound at once. Each one has its own distinct sound. For a few moments there is intensive calling, answering, beeping and dialing.

Bin-Bin   Five, three, seven, seven, zero, eight, eight, zero. That means "I think kiss kiss you hold hold you." Oh, you are too much. *(She enters a new code.)* Zero, five, six, zero, five, six.

Shih-Wen   *(Reading the message)* How can she say this? "You're boring, you're boring!" How can she say this to me?

Bin-Bin   *(Tired of the game, talking to herself.)* It's too much to talk to one another like this. Maybe we should just pick up the telephone. *(She places a three-way call to Rei-Chi and Shih-Wen.)* Wei?

Shih-Wen   Hello.

Rei-Chi   Moshi moshi.

Bin-Bin   Rei-Chi, did you finish all the homework already and then think of me?

Rei-Chi   Yeah—what are you doing right now?

Bin-Bin   Trying to read those chapters in Chemistry!

Rei-Chi   Oh, Chemistry! I almost forgot! You know, I just learned that new song from Namie Amuro.[7]

Bin-Bin	Really? Cool!!!
Rei-Chi	It's called "Wata Shi Wa Shin Ji De Su."
Bin-Bin	Will you teach it to me tomorrow after school?
Rei-Chi	No problem!
Bin-Bin & Rei-Chi	Shih-Wen? What are you doing right now?
Shih-Wen	I'm thinking about something important.
Rei-Chi	Oh, yeah? I thought you were fixing your father's old reading glasses.
Shih-Wen	Don't pick on me! Tell me what you are doing.
Rei-Chi	I'm reading a book of poetry.
Shih-Wen	Oh, poetry. How about this? "In the night, bathed in moonlight/ Seeing my childhood dreams fade away/ I find no desire to be a dragonfly anymore."
Bin-Bin	Is that your way of saying "farewell to my childhood?"
Rei-Chi	Bin-Bin, please listen to this one "Don't write your diary as if it were an accounting book/ Rather fill all its pages with feelings/ Passions jammed together and smeared with sweat and tears." (Thinking out loud) Oh, did I get that on my computer? Well, it doesn't

---

[7] Pronounced "nah-mee-ah" "ah-moo-row" with equal accents on all syllables.

matter. (Continuing with the poem.) "In pages upon pages/ Tears wash the paper in colors from light blue to dark blue./ These are words for longing/ For sharing the feelings of the heart."

Bin-Bin   Oh, I read that one too! Let me read one for you: "What would I do if I could not see you/ At the time of my most beautiful moment?/ Perhaps I will change myself into a tree/ Where I can stand on the sidewalk/ Patiently waiting for the moment you will pass by."

Rei-Chi   "Perhaps I will change myself into a tree, where I can stand on the sidewalk, patiently waiting for the moment you will pass by."

Music fades in, as the teenagers talk away, but can no longer be heard. As the lights fade to black, the music is up full and the scene is changed. Four small round tables are set up across the stage area. Each has three chairs. These are the tables in the photo shop where clients will sit to select their photo packages or review the contact sheets of their photo sessions.

Act I, Scene 7
A Once-In-A-Lifetime Occasion

The four tables are set up down right, down right of center, down left of center, and down left. As the lights come up, the music changes to a cheery Taiwanese folk song, played in Baroque style by an orchestra. As each pair of customers enters the shop, the sales staff will enter to greet them and take them to a table. The first couple enters. She (woman #1) is dressed conservatively in a pretty, long skirt. Perhaps she is an elementary school teacher. He (man #1) is a young man wearing his R.O.C. military uniform. They enter stage left and cross to down left center.

Sales 1	Why are you just standing at the gate? Come on in, it's all right to look.
Woman #1	*(They come into the reception area)* Is it okay?
Man #1	We just want to look around and compare the prices.
Andy	Welcome! Please come in and sit down! Our prices are not the lowest on Chungshan North Road, but we are not expensive–if you shop around, you'll see that is true.
Woman #1	Yes, we just want to look at many different bridal

salons.

Andy	But what's the use of comparing prices? Do you know what you are comparing?

Andy guides them down right to sit at the table there. Andy and salesclerk #1 sit with them. The second couple (woman and man #2) enters from stage right and moves to sit at the table down right center. They are a bit older, more sophisticated than the first couple. Salesclerk #2 welcomes them; she shows them a sample photo album.

Sales 2	These are some samples of our work. Please take a look. We have a lot of different settings: the European Garden, a Roman fountain, a lovely forest glen. But some couples like our more "avant garde" choices: the Superman setting or Jurassic Park.
Woman #2	Oh, really?!! Do you also have a Godzilla setting?
Sales #2	Of course we do! Whatever you want. We also have very special "Mulan" set. We even have Adam and Eve in the Garden of Eden!
Woman #2	And all these photos are taken in the studio?
Sales 2	Yes, we believe it's better to shoot them here than out on location.

Man #2	Would you mind telling us what sort of costumes Adam and Eve wear?
Sales 2	The design for them is very special! Adam wears tiny, leopard skin briefs and Eve wears a little bikini adorned with two shells. *(She makes a gesture to indicate that the shells cover the breasts.)*
Sales 6	*(Clerk has walked over to their table during the previous conversation.)* If that sort of costume doesn't appeal to you, how about "Snow White and the Seven Dwarfs"? So you have seven flower girls and seven attendants.
Woman #2	Oh, really? *(They look at the pictures.)*

At the table down right.

Andy	If you want my personal opinion about this company, I think the professionalism of our stylists and designers is unparalleled.
Sales 1	For example, you have probably heard of Andy. He's the hottest stylist on Chungshan North Road.
Woman #1	I think I saw his picture and a story of him in New Bridal News Magazine.

Sales 1	*(Gesturing to Andy)* So, don't you think he looks familiar to you?
Woman #1	Oh, it's you! You're Andy!
Andy	Oh, well...do you know that if you look at too many bridal gowns, it will really make your head spin? At a moment like this it's best for me to make the decision for you and to create a total head-to-toe look just for you.

A young couple has entered and they are seated at the down left table with Jeff.

Jeff	So at six A.M. you must get everything ready and be prepared to leave for the photo shoot.
Woman #3	Oh, six o'clock??? That's so early!
Jeff	If you think that's too early, then we have a very special package just for you. Our company has a country house in the Ta Hsi, especially for taking bridal photos.
Woman #3	*(excited)* Oh! Is that in mountainside estates?
Jeff	Well, sort of, sort of. You could say that. We go the night before. We'll take you in a Cadillac limousine,

so the next morning you don't have to get up so early for the photo shoot!

Woman & Man #3	Oh! A Cadillac! A Cadillac!
Man #3	Is there anything we need to bring ourselves?
Jeff	If you don't mind the trouble, you can bring anything that is special to you—a memento or gift—like your first love letter or a favorite Valentine's Day card, or that tie you wore on your first date.
Woman #3	Oh! I know! *(She whispers to the man.)*
Man #3	*(Enthusiastically)* The condom we used the first time!

Woman #3 hits him and they laugh; Jeff laughs as well. Meanwhile, the fourth couple enters and sits down at the down left center table. Salesclerk #3 greets them.

Sales 3	You must be the couple from Malaysia. Are you from Sarawak or Penang?
Woman & Man #4	We are from Penang.
Sales 6	*(Joining them at the table.)* Well, you came the right place. Coming back to Taiwan to take your bridal photos is a lifetime dream come true. Every spring

and autumn we have so many tour groups from near-
by countries—bringing so many couples here for their
photos.

Man #4   But we are just a group of two. We'd like to take our
time.

Sales 3   That's even better. Our photographers are the best.
Our quality is guaranteed.

At the table down right.

Sales 1   Absolutely! Our photographers are in great demand!
Other shops are always trying to hire them away.

Andy   If you aren't satisfied with the pictures we take, we'll
do another shoot until you are satisfied.

Man #1   But has anybody ever asked to have their photos re–
done?

Sales 1   Well, no—that hasn't happened yet.

Andy   But I think this lady is so beautiful that, whatever picture we take, you will certainly look wonderful in it.

Sales 1   Don't worry about it! There's absolutely no problem.
(Lowering her voice, confidentially.) Actually, I'm glad
you're not that kind of customer who always expects

an extra-added free gift for every little thing. That's why I say this to you. *(She moves in closer.)*

Andy   Really, you don't have to shop any more. It will just tire you out!

At the table down left.

Jeff   The country house is really fun, but you have to be careful and not stay up too late. You also don't want to drink too much water; otherwise your eyes will be puffy in the morning. Also, don't get too excited overnight, if you understand what I'm talking about!

Sales 6   *(Speaking to the woman)* No! You don't want to tire yourself out and get those awful black circles under your eyes!

At the table down left center, the couple there is reviewing the contact sheets of their previous photo shoot.

Woman #4   Oh, these turned out really nice! Which ones shall I choose?

Sales 3   Your bridal photos are a once-in-a-lifetime experience, so you must be very, very careful. Take your time while selecting your pictures. Don't pick any one that you are not fully satisfied with and—most importantly—don't overlook any good ones.

Woman #4   But we've already selected 36. If I choose anymore, we'll be over the number included in the package.

Man #4   Yeah. What do we do if we want more than that?

Sales 6   There will be no problem at all. For those you choose beyond the limit, I'll give you a 20% discount on the price. It was 850 NT per print.[8] Oh, maybe I have another deal for you! You can pick even more and I will throw in another present—I'll give you a second beautiful photo album that you can fill up with pictures and give to your mother. I believe you want to leave something for your own family, right! Remember, it's a once-in-a-lifetime occasion, so treat yourself generously.

Man #4   *(Joking)* So I should come again?

Woman #4   And just who do you want to come with the next time?

---

[8] "NT" stands for New Taiwanese dollars—about $25-27 U.S. This is pronounced "N" "T."

Man #4   If there is another time, of course I'll come with you!

At the table down left.

Woman #3   Let's see—we have three evening gowns and one
                Chinese gown and one Japanese-style dress.[9] Do you
                have all the different shoes to match them?

Jeff   No. Shoes should be part of your own trousseau. You
                have to provide them yourself.

Woman #3   Really? I have to buy all those shoes?

Jeff   You know, the word for shoes in Chinese is
                "hsieh" —it sounds just like the Chinese word for
                "harmony." So it's important to have as much harmo-
                ny as you can.

Woman #3   Is that true? Harmony, harmony, harmony — "hsieh"
                means harmony!

---

[9] A typical bridal shop order would be three gowns for the engagement party and
three for the wedding. The engagement gowns might be formal wear or in special
styles (such as Japanesedress, ancient Chinese dress, or "fantasy" clothing.) The
order would also include three dresses for the wedding day: a modern white
bridal gown, a gown for visiting each guest's table and toasting them, and a third
gown for seeing the guests off. As the engagement and wedding feasts continue,
the bride changes into this succession of dresses and is applauded at each
entrance in a new gown.

Man#3   It's all right. We can go shopping for shoes tomorrow.

At the table down left center.

Woman #4   I still want to have photographs taken on our wedding
             day.

Sales 2   You want to take pictures on your wedding day? Not
             very many people do that.

Man #4   So what you're saying is that taking the pictures of the
             bride and getting married are two entirely different
             things?

Sales 2   Yes, let me explain: getting married is the banquet
             business. You have thirty, forty, even fifty tables of
             guests eating, drinking and talking. They don't even
             have a chance to look at the bride. But your photo-
             graphs are a permanent memory—a beautiful record
             of a once-in-a-lifetime event. So the bride should con-
             sider this and treat herself well. Come, let me show
             you some dresses.

She takes them to see the dresses.
At the table down right.

Andy	Our company's system is the best. We never surprise you with surcharges or hidden costs. You can feel secure about that. And also, you know other companies sometimes ask our photographers to create sample photos for them. Those shops can show you very good sample photos, but what they actually produce are really poor.
Sales 1	Those terrible pictures are then left in the customers houses. Our shop is the only one that dares to show you the actual contact sheets. And these sheets here are just the rejects—the ones the customers didn't choose. They took the best ones with them.
Andy	Other companies would never dare to show you these.

At the table down left.

Jeff	*(Talking to himself at first.)* Do you know that for only a few thousand NT dollars, we are actually performing an extraordinary service for new couples? First, you come to us for a free consultation. Then you choose the clothes for the photo shoot. After we make alterations so the fit is just right, you pick up the

clothes. Then we meet with you to advise you before the photo shoot. Then we do the actual shoot. Then you pick out the wedding gowns. Then you come back to see the contact sheets and choose which ones you want developed and, of course, those photos you want enlarged. And for all these many services, I only get maybe one thousand or two thousand NT. So don't worry about anything. We have a special relationship with our customers. Just put your trust in me.

At the table down left center.

Man #4　　　　How about the photo negatives? We live so far away, in Malaysia. If we want to get more photos copied, we'd have to fly back here.

Woman #4　　　How about this...do you think you could let us have some of the negatives?

Sales 3　　　　Well, let me think about it. You know, nobody ever gives away the photo negatives. Maybe I can discuss this with the manager. *(She crosses to Jeff, they talk and he nods.)* Oh, since you have come from so far away and we like each other so much, I think I can give you

	a few of the negatives.
Man #4	Thank you, so we can develop what we like at home. Sort of a DIY project!
Man & Woman #4	DIY! DIY![10]

At the table down right center.

Sales 2	You know, in this profession, we raise our prices twice a year. That's why all our young couples want to place their orders as soon as possible. Because if you wait just two years it will cost you twenty or thirty thousand N.T. more!
Woman #2	This is such a good deal! And so romantic too!
Andy	Of course, the best in the world.
Sales 2	And don't you know that so many people want to get married by the end of this year, or at the beginning of the next because of the millennium frenzy. You are such a wise and beautiful lady. I think that today you will make the wisest decision.

---

[10] "DIY" is an expression for ' "do it yourself" —a very popular pastime in Taiwan. The characters also do a gesture here, mimicking a DIY television commercial: they press their palms together and rotate the fanned fingers back and forth, keeping the fingers flat and spread open.

Man #2 and Woman #2 leave.

At the table down left center.

Sales 3   Yes, we can say the European fashion is on the cutting edge, but talking about bridal fashions, no place compares to Taiwan. Our bridal design is the best in the world. When we talk about the variety of wedding dresses, those European designers are left speechless.

By now most of the customers have left and the staff begins cleaning up and moving out the added tables.

Sales 6   And the bridal salons in Mainland China are now learning from Taipei. In Beijing there is a big shop called Taiwan Bridal Salon. And there's one in Shanghai. Taiwanese businessmen have made all the investments and developed those businesses. And they have made millions!

Andy   And there's a shop in Szechwan opened by one of my cousins.

Sales 3   As a matter of fact, the bridal fashion and bridal photography in Taipei is the real "Taiwan Experience."

As the last tables and chairs are moved off, the salesclerks exit and music comes up and lights change.

Act I, Scene 8
Grandmother Jun-Mei's Story

Lights come up on Jun-Mei and her friend, Granny Plum, entering from down left. Jun-Mei is in her 80s and Plum is in her 70s. They both carry a bag of colorful clothes.

Pei-Pei   *(Off left)* Granny, I'm going to park the car. Can you carry all the clothes all right?

Jun-Mei   It's okay. I can even carry more. I was even going to ride here on Granny Plum's motorcycle.

Pei-Pei   Really? You're Wonder Woman!

Plum   That's nothing. Last time when we went to the Activity Center out in Taipei County, we rode on my cycle.

Jun-Mei   Yes, and the time we went all the way to Keelung too. *(Calling offstage to Pei-Pei)* Ay, Pei-Pei, we'll wait here for you. *(To Plum)* Hey, do you think they won't mind just to alter these dresses for us?

Plum   I think it's no problem. Last time they altered one for me. I don't think they'll mind—*(confidentially)*—especially in times of recession like this and since this is not an auspicious year for weddings. Besides I think they are so many bridal shop businesses, I imagine they don't mind making money anyway they can.

Jun-Mei   Okay, but it wouldn't hurt to ask them first.

Pei-Pei enters and crosses to the women to help them with the bags.

Jun-Mei   Hey, Pei-Pei! How come your pictures got developed
               so fast?
Pei-Pei   No, they aren't developed yet. I just came to take a
               look first. I didn't want mother to find me here. So
               don't you tell her!

Jun-Mei and Granny Plum exchange glances and smile.

Jun-Mei   Why would I want to tell her?

They enter the bridal salon.

Plum   Does that mean you took those R-rated or boudoir photos?

Jun-Mei   If you did, you can show them to us. It will be all right with us.

Pei-Pei   Amah! Grandma! No!!

She whispers to Jun-Mei and Granny Plum listens in. Surprised, the grannies exchange looks. They go into the salon and the salesclerks bring them two albums of snapshot size photo samples. Pei-Pei begins looking over the albums.

Plum   *(Looking at the albums)* These both look okay. This one is handsome. This one is kind of sincere, but also cute.

Jun-Mei   Is that because you don't like the one your mother picked?

Pei-Pei   No, I didn't say that. Oh, grandmother, do all girls have to get married someday?

On the next two lines, the grannies intone and use gestures from Taiwanese Opera. Jun-Mei uses the woman's gesture, Plum uses the man's.

Jun-Mei   For this matter...

Plum	For this matter...
Jun-Mei	*(In normal voice)* For this matter, I don't want to give you "black-and-white" talk. Your mother will get angry. I think getting married...yes, it is better.
Plum	Getting married is better, if you go into it with your eyes open!
Jun-Mei	You can't always tell a book by its cover.
Plum	Some people have an easy personality before marriage but after getting married they completely change.
Jun-Mei	Just find somebody you feel is right for you.
Plum	If you can't find him, don't get married.

Jun-Mei sees the wig on the mannequin.

Jun-Mei	Hey, that wig looks exactly like the hairstyle I use to wear when I was a little girl. *(She starts to try it on.)*
Sales 3	Yes, lady, do you want to try it on?
Plum	*(Looking at the photos.)* These two boyfriends—you don't want either of them? I don't believe you! If you don't want them, why did you come and take these beautiful, romantic pictures? Who do you want to

show them to?

Pei-Pei	*(She smiles at Plum and speaks to Jun-Mei)* Granny, why did you decide to marry grandfather? What was your reason?
Sales 3	This is your grandmother? How wonderful! Oh, grandmother, would you like to try on this dress as well?
Sales 1	This suit has just arrived. We'd really like to have someone model it for us!

The clerks take Jun-Mei behind the screen to change into the suit.

Pei-Pei	Grandmother, how old were you when you got married?

As she dresses, Jun-Mei pokes her head around the screen to talk to Pei-Pei.

Jun-Mei	Me? When I was a young girl, I never thought about getting married. When I finished public school I really wanted to try and get into middle school. At that time Taiwan only had one middle school for girls: the Third High School. And I made it!

Sales 1	What is the Third High School now?
Sales 6	Chungshan Girl's High.
Plum	Oh, at that time she was really outstanding. She was a top-notch student leader. In science and math she always made straight A's. And in piano and painting and even track she got first prize! When she graduated our principal thought she would apply to the medical school in Japan.

By this time Jun-Mei has changed into the suit. It's like a modern suit with a light-colored jacket with a Mandarin collar; the skirt is dark, pleated. It is subtly like the fashion for schoolgirls at that time. The wig is a black "China Doll" cut. Jun-Mei comes out and crosses down to the downstage edge of the salon platform. Jun-Mei walks, slowly, remembering.

Jun-Mei	But after I graduated from high school there were many matchmakers sent to my house by wealthy families. My diploma raised my currency as a potential bride.
Sales 6	I know the engagement money was very important in those days. The girls who graduated from that high school were worth six thousand in gold. And the students from the private girls' school Jinshio were worth

three thousand in gold. Even those girls who graduat-
ed from public school could ask for one thousand in
gold.

Sales 3   Not just that. I knew there were many girls worth ten
thousand, even twenty thousand in gold at that time.

*During this conversation, Jun-Mei leaves them, going downstage on the
platform. A spotlight on stage left comes up to reveal Jun-Mei's high school
principal. He wears a formal uniform in Japanese style.*

Jun-Mei   I just feel very depressed and hurt because I cannot go
to Japan. *(She lifts up her head.)* Mr. Principal, I want
to...study medicine.

Principal   *(Japanese accent)* Oh, Miss Jun-Mei. You study medicine? Your school credit looks very good but in
Taiwan, if you're a girl who wants to study medicine—
well, it's not possible. However, I think by the time
you want to go I could write you a letter of recom-
mendation for study in Japan. And you can get into
the two-year chemistry program for basic training.
After that you can apply to the Tokyo Girls Special
Medical College. Would your family have the means

	and money for you to go there?
Jun-Mei	My mother passed away a long time ago and my second mother would not spare the money for me to go there. And my father would not let me... *(She drops her head, unable to continue.)*
Principal	Well, is that so? Then what will you do after you graduate? I thought you would continue...*(He sighs and starts to leave.)* So much promise...*(He exits.)*
Jun-Mei	*(Lifting her head)* I turned away those matchmakers sent by those wealthy families. And I started seeing the cousin of my classmate. *(Her face beams.)* He wrote me letters and I gave them to my father to read. My father was a little angry. But I wouldn't look at any of the rich boys, because I was afraid I wouldn't be able to share ideas with those sons—their personalities weren't good. So finally I told my father I didn't care about getting any dowry. So my family gave in and let me choose my own husband.[11]
Sales 1	We know at that time there were already people wearing western style white wedding gowns. What did you wear?
Jun-Mei	*(Laughs)* What did I wear? I wore something almost

like this and put a big red shawl on my shoulders. And I carried a pair of new pillows with lovebirds embroidered on them. That was my second mother's gift to me. And a basket full of chicken eggs. I walked from my father's house to my husband's house.

Sales 3 　Is that so? No horns, no gongs, and no flowered sedan chair for the bride? You just walked over there? I can't believe that your husband's family was really serious about the wedding.

Sales 6 　(To sales 3) I don't think you should say that. (To Jun-Mei and Pei-Pei) We just feel curious, that's all. We didn't know that your grandmother was such a modern woman back then.

Sales 1 　Oh no, I just feel bad because otherwise we could see grandmother's wedding pictures. I've seen some old

---

[11] During the next speeches, Jun-Mei sat and Sales3 went through the motions of preparing the face of the bride for her make-up on her wedding day. This specific business involved Sales3 taking a cotton thread, hooking the middle of the thread in her teeth and pulling the ends of the thread taut and twisting them together, then pulling them across Jun-Mei's face to pull out small facial hairs. This traditional "Chinese facial" was done to prepare the face for the bridal make-up—the first make-up she would have worn. The director may choose to substitute this business with another action, such as placing flowers in Jun-Mei's hair. The important thing is to subtly set the scene for Jun-Mei's memory of her wedding day.

wedding photos and the hairdo's were all so...

Pei-Pei	But grandmother, how do you feel about it? Looking back, do you regret it?
Jun-Mei	It was the way we wanted it. I myself never felt any regrets because we wanted the parents from both sides to agree. We had waited a long time. But after I got married there were so many things I had wanted to do, but I could not do them anymore. And life was really very hard. Things never happen like you wish them to. And we both even thought what fools we were. Yes, even your grandfather sometimes thought so.

She begins to remember and her husband appears, dressed as a young intellectual in a youth organization uniform. He enters slowly and kneels to the left of her. She also kneels, Japanese style. He is seen finishing reading a book, then he looks up and sighs.

Husband	I think I only want a career in literature, I don't want any children.
Jun-Mei	When I first heard him say that I was astonished.
Husband	But I don't think we can get away without having any. So maybe we'll just have one, first.

Jun-Mei	Then I knew I had been taken in.
Husband	If the first one is a girl, then we'll have another one. Maybe we'll have three and then think about it.
Jun-Mei	If all three are girls you cannot ask me to have another one.
Husband	Of course. By that time you can decide.
Jun-Mei	*(Turns away a bit from him and says to the audience)* At that time the husbands were willing to discuss matters like this before marriage. It was very nice. How could I know that later he just would want to keep going. *(She's a little embarrassed to say this.)*
Husband	*(He moves close, speaking intimately to her.)* You can't blame me for all this. We didn't make a sworn statement or write it down and seal the agreement. *(Jun-Mei turns away from him.)* When you told me, I agreed. I didn't think we would... I mean, it was so easy for us to have children.

He slowly puts his head on her shoulder. She takes her hand and caresses his cheek. After a pause, they move apart and she rises.

Jun-Mei	During those times I tried to avoid pregnancy but did-

n't know how. It was not like now—children just came, year after year. I slowly forgot almost anything—piano, painting—my fingers became like ten dry sticks. Only on the day of my wedding can I say I was the modern girl. I was intellectually advanced. I thought I was emulating some great revolutionary. But in reality I learned how to raise children, wash clothes and diapers, how to start a fire in the stove and cook all those meals. During that time life was very difficult. Adults and children all got sick so easily and every child is hard to bring up.

As she speaks, Jun-Mei slowly pulls down her scarf and twists it into a shape that becomes a baby she cradles in her arms. She puts the "baby" on her shoulder, patting to stop its crying. Her husband slowly rises, crosses to her. She gives the "baby" to him. They cross a bit upstage. He gives it to one of the salesclerks. Before this the clerks had been continuing their shop work. Now the "baby" is passed from one to the next as a moving Taiwanese cradlesong is heard. The baby is carried out. The lights fade out, leaving Jun-Mei remembering her life.

The lights come up down right to pick up Bin-Bin and Shih-Wen who will cross over to down left during these speeches.

Bin-Bin   You know in my grandmother's time medicine, hygiene, nutrition and genetics were not very well developed. My grandmother had eleven children! Oh, heavens, how tired she was. How hard it was for her. And now only the third, the seventh, and the eleventh of those children are still here! My mother was the seventh and is the only remaining daughter. Of course, she was not sold to any other people's house. And no matter how hard it was my grandmother let my mother continue her studies. She even sent my mother to the best school where she got a higher degree even than my uncles.

Jun-Mei   *(A salesclerk assists Jun-Mei in changing back into her own clothes.)* Oh, now it's so different. My oldest son has three children, my daughter only two. The younger son said he only wants one! Oh, it's okay. It's all very good.

Sales 6   Now everybody has plans and in our business the clerks plan their pregnancies according to our high and low seasons.

Sales 1	And have you noticed, all the girls here prefer daughters. Most of them have daughters too.
Sales 3	Isn't that because everybody looks at these beautiful wedding gowns, so everybody turns soft and romantic?
Sales 6	I'm really glad I'm in this career—this beauty career!
Jun-Mei	*(Walking through them.)* I think the girl has to have her own future. Those who are capable should work and fulfill their own potential. I don't think a girl should get married and just rely on the husband. That's nothing.
Pei-Pei	Oh, grandma, do you think getting married later is better? Or is it better not to get married at all?
Jun-Mei	No, I didn't say anything about getting married later. I didn't say anything about not getting married either.
Plum	You girls can go ahead and get married. We don't need to get married anymore.

Rei-Chi joins Bin-Bin and Shih-Wen.

Rei-Chi	I think having babies is just horrible. Today many people say they don't want to have children.

Bin-Bin	If everybody decided not to have children, then we wouldn't be here!
Rei-Chi	But it hurts so much! Oh, maybe adoption would be nice. To adopt or have your own—it doesn't make any difference.
Shih-Wen	How about if there's a kid that looks like yourself. For example, *(pointing to them)* it has your eyebrows and your eyes, your lips and your nose, and both of your cheeks. Wouldn't it be lovely? I don't see why you wouldn't like it.
Rei-Chi	Oh, I like that. Bin-Bin, so that means we still have to have our own baby. So what should we do?
Shih-Wen	Since science is so developed, I believe there must be a way to give birth without pain or problems.
Bin-Bin	Maybe we can have a test tube baby! But we still need a person's body. Oh, I've got it! We can be cloned.
Rei-Chi	Cloned? But producing a clone would create a baby exactly like you. Then we cannot have a baby that looks like both you and me.
Shih-Wen	And like me!
Rei-Chi	*(Speaking in "beeper code")* Zero five six! Zero five six! You are too much!
Shih-Wen	What's wrong with the baby looking like me too? I mean

	if the baby will look like Bin-Bin and you, don't you think there's a way to have a child look like all three of us?
Bin-Bin	Hmmm. I believe there must be a way. Let me go through my mother's bookshelves to see if I can find an article about that. Probably many human beings all over the world are trying to invent this technique.

The lights go down on Bin-Bin and friends and come up in the bridal shop. Jun-Mei has now changed back onto her regular clothes.

Jun-Mei	*(To Salesclerk 1)* Thank you for all your nice words to me. You liked the dress I put on, right? So is that from your period collection of dresses?
Sales 1	Oh, you looked so very nice in it. We didn't know that those earlier brides would wear only that for the wedding. *(Sweetly)* Thank you for trying it out for us. We will let the costumers for the period collection know how the dress was worn and the special charm of the brides of that time.
Plum	You talked such a long time and you never even mentioned our skirts!
Jun-Mei	*(Laughing loudly)* Oh, yes. I forgot! It must be the Alzheimer's!

Everyone laughs with her. Plum and Jun-Mei take out their skirts.

Jun-Mei	Hey girls. How about altering these dancing gowns for us? Maybe not alter—just enlarge them. Enlarge them so all the grandmothers can wear them.
Sales 6	Do all these belong to you?
Jun-Mei	These belong to our Senior Citizen group, the Evergreen Ballroom Dance Troupe.
Plum	We are planning to go abroad for the ballroom competition so we want to use these for our weekly practice. These dresses are donated from the Lions' Club so they didn't cost us a penny! So maybe you can give us a discount on the alterations?
Pei-Pei	And maybe in the future when they go to the contest they will ask you to design their formal costumes.
Sales 6	Okay, we'll do it for you. Please take all these to the third floor and talk to our seamstress.

Plum and Jun-Mei ad lib "*Okay, thank you so much.*" "*I'm so glad they don't mind...*" *etc. The lights go down in the shop as they exit. At the same time the lights come up upstage left where the teenagers are checking out several large books and academic papers.*

Rei-Chi	Then how about two females? Can they produce a baby?
Bin-Bin	Yes, but only if we can make the two embryos grow together.
Rei-Chi	How about two males? Can they produce a baby?
Bin-Bin	Of course they can. I think.
Shih-Wen	How about two females and a male? Can they produce a baby?
Bin-Bin	Yes because it is one sperm and two eggs.
Shih-Wen	Then who wants to be the one to get pregnant?

Bin-Bin and Rei-Chi look at each other and turn serious.

Bin-Bin	*(Elbowing Rei-Chi)* How about you?
Rei-Chi	*(Elbowing Bin-Bin)* How about you?
Bin-Bin	You!
Rei-Chi	You!
Shih-Wen	How about me?

Bin-Bin and Rei-Chi look at him, staring.

Shih-Wen	*(Stepping back)* I'm willing to do it if I can.

Bin-Bin tosses the books to Rei-Chi and chases Shih-Wen across the upstage area. She jumps on his back and he carries her off stage left, followed by Rei-Chi.

Act I, Scene 9
Pei-Pei's Nightmare

Lights come up on Pei-Pei, alone in the salon. She is seated, her head thrown back as though asleep. Suddenly she sits upright, kicking off her shoes.

Pei-Pei   Grandmother! You guys say you never want to get married again. Why should I go into a marriage? *(She stands, looking at the big photo albums on the table.)* Oh! Getting married! Then one can never do the things one wants to do. *(She looks at a photo of two "lovebirds.")* Maybe after marriage there's no love anymore. Marriage is just the day-to-day routine. *(She sits down, picking up several albums at once.)* Getting married is supposed to mean marrying someone you really love. But ten years...twenty years...thirty years...! *(She begins to leave the shop, carrying all the albums she can, weighed down by them.)* Ten years...twenty years...thirty years...! Unless...

Pei-Pei sighs and turns around to see her mother, Jin-Hua, appear stage left.

Pei-Pei	Oh, mother! This is horrible! I'm so scared. Mother, do you know just how terrible this is? I don't dare to think about it.
Jin-Hua	What's the matter, Pei-Pei? Tell me about it.
Pei-Pei	I can't tell you yet.
Jin-Hua	Oh, Pei-Pei. You look like something's wrong with you.
Pei-Pei	Me? Oh, I'm just a little confused.

Hsiao-Chou and Tony appear upstage. They stand behind scrim in the portals of the back wall of the reception area. As the lights come up to reveal them, they are seen wearing formal suits, so they look like grooms in wedding photos. Pei-Pei looks at them as if they are pictures in the album.

Jin-Hua	Is that because he *(she points to Tony)* makes you confused about him *(she points to Hsiao-Chou)*?
Pei-Pei	No, because of me—myself. And because of you, my mother.
Jin-Hua	No, don't blame it on me. When you grow up, when you mature to the extent that you don't blame your

	mother for everything—that's when you will be ready for marriage.
Hsiao-Chou	Pei-Pei is such a romantic!
Tony	Pei-Pei is very smart.
Hsiao-Chou	I want to marry a girl like this. She's so capable and lovely. Just like her mother—my mother-in-law!
Tony	*(Laughing loudly.)* Just like your mother-in-law?
Pei-Pei	Mother, do you hear that?
Jin-Hua	*(Smiling and turning to the front.)* We've been trying so hard all our lives...

Hsio-Jen appears up right in front of the dressing mirror. Jun-Mei comes from upstairs. As she slowly comes down, Jun-Mei and Hsio-Jen look at each other.

Jin-Hua	*(She looks at Jun-Mei, then back to the front, continuing her thought.)*...to make it possible for our daughter not to be just like us...

Jin-Hua slowly looks to Pei-Pei who starts to run offstage with the albums; she runs awkwardly as Jin-Hua picks up her shoes and follows after her. Hsio-Jen disappears and Jun-Mei slowly begins to leave the shop. As she slowly exits, the lights change.

Up-tempo, happy music is heard as couples and groups of customers dance in and across the stage. They dance and look at dresses, pantomiming conversations with the sales staff. The dance builds to a climax when one customer, who is trying on a long gown and high heels, gets to center stage and trips and falls. All the customers stop, shocked, watching her. She is caught in a spotlight. Andy steps forward and tries to help her up. She falls again as the lights go out, last of all the spot on the fallen bride goes dark.

End of Act One

ActII

Act II, Scene 1
The Evergreen Ballroom Dance Troupe

As the curtain rises, we hear a Strauss waltz and see silhouettes of couples dancing. The lights come up quickly as the music peaks. Four elderly couples are discovered, the women dressed in the gowns Jun-Mei had in I-8. Jun-Mei dances with Granny Plum. A coach instructs the dancers: "Faster!" "Now turn." etc. Two couples collide on a fast turn. One elderly man is struck on the leg.

Old man 1	Ow!
Jun-Mei	Oh, does it hurt? Coach, can we let him take a little rest, drink some tea?
Old man 2	No, don't rest! We can't take a break because all those guys from the Tai Chi Group will be here soon. They've booked the space.
Old lady 1	I'm so sorry. It's my fault. I made the mistake. Next time, I'll remember!
Coach	Next time? Next time! We have no next time. Next time we'll be performing at the Community Center.
Old lady 1	Oh really? *(She pulls herself together, trying to get the*

step right.)

Jun-Mei	Isn't there a performance for the Veteran's Association?
Plum	It's the fifth of next month.
Old man 1	What? What? Where?
Jun-Mei & Plum	*(Shouting, as he is hard of hearing)* Veteran's Association —next month.
Plum	Still, next month is not far away.
Old man 1	Jun-Mei, by the way, aren't you going to ask us to perform at your granddaughter's wedding? Or maybe your were just kidding us?
Jun-Mei	I wasn't kidding. It's a real invitation.
Old man 3	When will that be?
Jun-Mei	Oh, she hasn't decided on the date yet.
Old lady 1	Didn't she already have her photos taken? And since she's done that, how can she not know when the wedding will be? *(Softly)* Is that because she doesn't want to tell you about it?
Old lady 2	I guess probably she didn't really want us old ladies to perform, but she didn't want to come out and say so. So she's telling her grandmother, *(mimicking a young girl)* "I haven't decided yet."

Jun-Mei is too embarrassed to speak, so Plum steps in.

Plum	No, no, it's not that. Young girls these days are all very busy. Maybe she doesn't have time to get married.
Jun-Mei	I think maybe for her...maybe it's really hard for her to make up her mind.
Plum	Okay, I'll ask her for you. If the grandmother asks her, a kid will just say "Pressure! Pressure again!" *(All the couples laugh in agreement.)*
Coach	Grandmas and grandpas! Please stop chatting! Come, let's practice once more. How about our favorite— tango! *(They assume tango positions.)* Beautiful, beautiful! Now make your bodies glide. Come, change the music. Let's just begin here, then dance through the trees and over there. There's more room over there.

The tango music comes on and the group begins the dance and dances offstage. Old man #2 is too slow, and the Coach stops him and dances off with him. Jun-Mei and Plum are the last couple. Plum dances the man's part as they tango offstage. The music fades out as the lights come up for the next scene.

Act II, Scene 2
Sad Stories at the Tiptop

As the lights come up in the shop, Andy is discovered looking at fashion magazines. Salesclerk #1 enters.

Sales 1   Andy, I want to talk to you about something. But don't tell the others, okay? *(Andy immediately looks interested.)* Promise me! Really! Don't tell anybody!

Andy   *(Joking)* Don't tell anyone? Oh, my god! You want to borrow money from me? Did you get cheated again? Did you make a bad loan?

Sales 1   Oh! Don't say things like that! I just want to talk to you seriously. And you always joke with me. Forget it. I don't want to talk to you anymore.

Andy   Okay, okay. I'm sorry. I'm listening. *(She doesn't speak.)* What happened? Are you pregnant?

Angry, salesclerk 1 gives Andy a look, then looks away.

Andy   Okay, I swear! No more jokes. *(He waits and she turns* *to him slowly.)*

Sales 1	I think I'm going to leave the shop. I will work to the end of this month. A friend of mine has asked me to open a studio with her.
Andy	Ah! Where did this friend come from?
Sales 1	Mmm...it's just someone I knew when I was studying design...
Andy	You want to open a shop yourself, huh?
Sales 1	It's not that. Last month you know my sales didn't reach the one million mark.
Andy	Oh, these last few months it has been kind of difficult. Even the customers are kind of different. They calculate more. And everybody feels the pressure—not just you.
Sales 1	The manager didn't really say anything to me, I just feel kind of bad. Every time I see a customer come in, I also see that customer walk out without signing a contract. No matter how hard I try, sometimes I feel so anxious I almost want to put a gun to their heads until they sign.
Andy	Well, in any business there are ups and downs. But don't think going out and opening your own shop is

any easier. Many people start up in this business—many people want to go into business for themselves. But they fail and have to come back and be a sales-clerk again. *(Batting his eyes at her.)* I was like that. I came back like a dog with my tail between my legs! In Taiwan there are more failed bridal shops than shops in operation. Really, don't go just yet. You can try a little longer.

Sales 1   *(Sighs)* If I continue like this I'll probably end up bor-rowing money from you.

Andy   Well, it's easier than getting pregnant!

Sales 2   *(Runs in excitedly)* Oh, I'm so sorry! I'm so sorry! A-Hao cannot come to work today. He has a bleeding ulcer! I just took him to the hospital!

Sales 1   What happened? How did he get that bad?

Sales 2   He was moonlighting every night—working on com-mercial shoots. He didn't pay any attention to his stomach aches.

Andy   How could he not pay attention to his life? How can anyone work two jobs, day and night?

Sales 2   I have to work extra. Otherwise, how can you make it? I have my wife and children to take care of. But I can't work like A-Hao—day and night, running around outside from one photo shoot to the next. It's all I can do to sit at the computer and do layout work. My wrists get so stiff from working the mouse!

Sales 1   *(Gives him a sympathetic look.)* No wonder all the photos you take look so unfocused.

Sales 2   Don't make jokes about that! I already got called on the carpet by the boss about that! So I always advise people not to get married too early.

Sales 1   Shhh! You can't say things like that in a bridal salon!

Sales 2   We can say anything here because it's true. The fact is, it's hard to make money when the kids are small and your wife can't work.

Sales 1   You knew that a long time ago so don't complain too much. But we know that A-Hao wants to get married. He wants to get married like crazy.

Andy   Oh yeah? I thought A-Hao and his girlfriend were quite serious. Aren't they living in an apartment in Jin-Mei?

Sales 2   Right! Near the college where they used to attend. They've lived there a long time.

Andy   So they are doing fine. What does he need to get married for?

Sales 1	Both of them work so hard and save money because they want to buy a house and get married.
Andy	Why?
Sales 1	So they feel more secure. They don't want the families to ask questions and keep pushing them and all that.
Sales 6	*(Enters sobbing.)* What's the use of having a house?
Sales 1	Oh, what's happened? You're...oh! Did your husband stay out again? *(Salesclerk 6 nods.)* How many days this time?
Sales 6	He didn't come back for more than a week. He called once to say he couldn't come back to us because that woman he's with took out a meat cleaver and threatened to kill herself!
Sales 1	Aaaah! What a mess!
Sales 2	That kind of husband, you're better off without him.
Andy	I wonder why he's not afraid that you'll take out a meat cleaver too? You can also make a scene, you know. Go to his office. Really! Go to his office—with the cleaver! *(He pushes Sales #1 towards Sales #6.)* You go with her.
Sales 1	Hey! Wait a minute! Why don't you go with her?

Andy	I can't. I don't want people to get the wrong idea about us.
Sales 1	I don't think they will get the wrong idea!
Andy	Shut up! *(To Salesclerk 6)* Come, come. Don't cry. *(Wiping her tears.)* You'll get your eyes all swollen. If a customer comes in they'll think something has happened here.
Sales 6	Okay. Oh, it's okay. Don't worry about me. *(Drying her eyes.)* No matter what my own problems are, I'll still give my best blessings to all those young lovers who want to get married.
Sales 1	I hope you feel better now. Later we can sign out early. I'll go pick up your daughter first and we'll all go get pizza together. This afternoon I think there are several groups of customers coming in to see their photos. Why don't we sort them out first?
Andy	What's wrong with this afternoon? People not showing up for work, you two wanting to get out early. Well, I'm going to take a swim. *(To Salesclerk 2)* Why don't you just have your own one-man show here? You've got the floor.
Sales 2	Am I the only one left here? How about Hsiao-Wu—is he still waiting for the photos?

Sales 6	No, no. They were ordered express. He got the shots back yesterday.
Sales 1	So maybe he went with Jeff to the World Trade Center? They have that planning session for the Bridal Gown Trade Show.
Andy	No, no, no. Jeff was driving his own car all by himself.
Sales 2	So where is Hsiao-Wu today? Oh, I know! He's been saying that he doesn't really want a wedding, he just wants to get a license and be married by a judge. Maybe he went today?
Sales 1	Today? Married by a judge? I don't believe it!
Andy	Oh, my god! What happened to him? Did anybody know about this?
Sales 1	What kind of friendship is that? He didn't say a word to us.
Sales 6	Doesn't he know the rules in our shop? All the employees get 60 percent off the cost. So it's a good deal to be married here. And we won't make money on him!
Sales 1	*(Joking.)* Oh, it's hard to say— "I won't make money on him."

Sales 2	And he has too many wrinkles! It would be difficult to airbrush them out of the shots!
Andy	And if we do get his photos all fixed, we can put them out front in the sample books. *(All laugh.)*
Sales 1	But I still don't believe he would just sneak off and get married like that. He said once he didn't want to get married.
Andy	Oh, he was just talking through his hat. Those people who keep saying, "I won't get married" are the very ones who get married very quickly. *(To salesclerk 1)* Look at you. What kind of face is that? Are you still angry? Don't worry. He'll be here soon. He can't afford to skip work. He's already earned a penalty this month for taking so many days off.
Sales 1	All right. I shouldn't be like this but I feel that anybody who doesn't want to get married in our shop is no friend of mine.

Act II, Scene 3
An Unexpected Meeting

Pei-Pei enters from stage left, walking towards the shop. Andy sees her and greets her. As he does so, Salesclerks 1 and 6 immediately brighten up and smile broadly.

Andy	Hello, Miss Pei-Pei! How are you?
Sales 1	Miss Pei-Pei, all your pictures are ready.

Salesclerk 6 takes several small albums of sample photos and meets Pei-Pei.

Sales 6	They're all here. Come, let me show you. Every single one is so pretty! It was a very successful photo session. Even our assistant said he never saw a session so perfect—without any "bloopers"!
Pei-Pei	Oh, really? Even when I was falling down? All those shots looked okay?
Sales 6	Yes, so darling! So cute!

Tony is seen crossing upstage, outside the shop. He whistles "Pretty Woman." As he crosses left, Pei-Pei sees him and runs to meet him outside the shop, under the tree.

Pei-Pei   Tony! You're back early!

Tony   Yes, I have something to tell you.

Pei-Pei   Good or bad? Let me guess. Your car was towed away? You want me to get it back? Or your credit card was stolen? Your passport disappeared? Or what?

Tony   No, no, no. None of that. I wish I could be that brainless. All right, I'll tell you. I have good news and bad news. Bad first. *(He takes on a serious expression.)* I quit smoking. *(Pei-Pei laughs.)* Quitting smoking is like taking everything away from me, especially those pleasures related to illusions: my postures, my gestures, my glances, my charm, and my attitude of carefree abandon—even my insistence that I'd rather die than change! But giving up smoking can make me reinvent myself so I can become Chou En Lai. I only need four hours sleep a day and I can play soccer again!

Pei-Pei   Really, it sounds like you had to make a tough choice.

	If that's the bad news, how about the good news?
Tony	Our proposal passed! Our design team won second place in the public art competition. We'll actually combine with the first team, so...
Pei-Pei	Two million and eight hundred thousand NT? *(He shakes his head "no.")* Five million?!! *(She pounces on him.)* Wow! That's great! No wonder you said the bad news was quitting smoking! This is really great. That's what the combined team will get for the whole project?

As Tony and Pei-Pei embrace and celebrate, Jin-Hua and Hsiao-Chou enter down right, outside the salon. Hsiao-Chou wears a fine suit and is chatting easily with Jin-Hua. The lights fade out on Tony and Pei-Pei.

Hsiao-Chou	My dear mother actually is quite anxious, but she doesn't want to push us. She adores Pei-Pei so she even treats me—her own son—extra politely! She always takes the long way around. She got my elder sister to ask me about the wedding plans. Mother even said she already has prepared the house for us.
	My mother likes Pei-Pei so much that whenever Pei-

Pei comes to Tainan my mother wants to invite guests for dinner every day. That's so our relatives and important friends can all meet Pei-Pei.

Lately mother bought new living room furniture so when you come down to Tainan for the banquet we will have good face.

Jin-Hua Ah! You've gone to so much trouble! This is too much! But I'm very touched by it. As for you, you do so much for Pei-Pei—I couldn't ask for better! But as for Pei-Pei herself, what's going on with her? I'm not quite sure. All of a sudden she'll act like a grown-up and the next moment she's like a child. But if you can take care of her, then I feel I won't have to worry anymore. But I should say that I believe there is something on her mind that she cannot resolve.

Hsiao-Chou Oh, for a young woman, when she thinks about leaving her parents' house, she'll be afraid. She feels it's not easy to leave. I will be very patient. *(Jokingly)* Isn't there a Taiwanese saying about a groom—something brave and naughty and kowtowing and adoring?

Jin-Hua Yes! The sixth is brave and the seventh is naughty and the eighth is...oh, you've heard that before. Let me think about it. What is the whole thing? Ah yes, a groom has to be, first: wealthy, second: lucky, third: handsome, fourth: young. *(She looks at him.)* You can't say you don't have those qualities. What's the fifth? Oh, the fifth is a groom must be brave, sixth is bold, *(Hsiao-Chou speaks with her)* seventh is naughty, eighth is unflappable, ninth is kowtowing to her every whim, and the tenth is adoring.

Jin-Hua is clearly delighted. The lights fade out on them and up on Pei-Pei and Tony.

Pei-Pei	Sometimes I feel that settling down might be rather odd because you have the same kind of life everyday.
Tony	If you are with me, then there'll be a great difference in night and day!
Pei-Pei	You! You sleep all day and go to bars all night!
Tony	Oh, you are much too nice. I'm probably in the bar all day too! No, no, it's not that great. I'm really busy and as tired as a dog. I have seven or eight days every month where I work without sleep and don't even get to the pub. And how about the rest of the time?

	(Speaking intimately) I'm always under surveillance by you!
Pei-Pei	*(Moving close, sweetly)* Not really. Will you love me like this forever?
Tony	I will love you.
Pei-Pei	But?
Tony	Not just like this. I am changing all the time and full of surprises.
Pei-Pei	I am changing all the time and full of tricks!
Tony	Just like these photos.
Pei-Pei	Do you like them? *(She shows him the albums.)*
Tony	Yes, I do.
Pei-Pei	Which one do you like best?
Tony	This one!
Pei-Pei	Me too. This is my favorite too! *(They embrace and kiss.)*
Tony	It's not that I don't want to marry you. One day we will have a complete closeness, one hundred percent—just like two hearts in one castle. But it's not that easy right now. Will you wait for a while? *(She gives him a look.)* You won't just go off and marry that guy with the Polo glasses and the YSL tie and his commute to

the Science and Technology Institute in Hsinchu, will you?

Pei-Pei   You know his mother has been pushing very hard.

Tony   You're not marrying his family.

Pei-Pei   And he goes out of his way to please my mother. She is absolutely delighted with everything he does.

Tony   *(Angry.)* Oh, shit! That's a low blow!

As Pei-Pei laughs, we see she is very happy. Meanwhile the lights come up again on Jin-Hua and Hsiao-Chou.

Hsiao-Chou   Naughty? Unflappable? Kowtowing and adoring? I can do all that. But you know taking the photos was all Pei-Pei's idea. I agreed to go along with it because, just like the clerk said, after the photo session the wedding date can't bc far away.

Today I troubled you to come to the salon so you can pick out the most beautiful photos for Pei-Pei and then we can decide on the material and style that would be best for her wedding gown. I think Pei-Pei wants to order an original dress of her own.

Jin-Hua   Yes, I think she does. Even with the two of you working, it's not easy. So I discussed it with her father. Now that you've had the photos and maybe you want to go to the beach or park for some other pictures, the cost will be considerable. Say 120,000 NT at least? Or even more? Let us older people pay the cost for you.

Hsiao-Chou   Oh, no, never! We don't want you to worry about this.

Jin-Hua   I talked to her father—everything is settled. Really!

Hsiao-Chou   Please! I believe Pei-Pei will agree with me.

Jin-Hua and Hsiao-Chou talk and move towards the shop.

Tony   Come on, let's get a special print made of our favorite photo.

As Tony and Pei-Pei move to enter the shop, they come face to face with Jin-Hua and Hsiao-Chou.

Jin-Hua   What is this all about?

Tony   What is this all about?

Hsiao-Chou   What is this all about?

Pei-Pei   What is this all about?

Sales 7   *(Greeting them with a poem)*

	A happy couple in such good fortune, Let your spirits rise and sail on!
Sales 6	Capture your joyful moment with us In special photos from our bridal salon!
Sales 7	Come inside, please sit down. Let's talk.
Sales 6	Would you like a glass of Icy Passion Fruit Tea? It's European style!

The four totally ignore the salesclerks.

Pei-Pei	Well, this is Tony. This is Hsiao-Chou. This is my mother. I came with both of them to the 21st Century Tiptop Bridal Salon and I took pictures on the Forever Love special photo offer. That's what this is all about. Did I do something terribly wrong? Was it really an unforgivable act?
Jin-Hua	Oh, no!
Tony	Oh, no!
Hsiao-Chou	Oh, no!
Pei-Pei	Then why are you all staring at me like that?
Hsiao-Chou	I wasn't staring at you, Pei-Pei.
Tony	I wasn't either, Pei-Pei.

Jin-Hua	Nor did I. Pei-Pei, come over here. Mother has something to say to you. *(She pulls Pei-Pei to one side.)* Come with me. Now look at me.
Tony	Pei-Pei, look at me. *(She does so.)*
Hsiao-Chou	Pei-Pei, look at me.

Pei-Pei looks at Hsiao-Chou, crosses to him and gives him a hug. Then she crosses to Tony and gives him a hug.

| Pei-Pei | I don't think you understand me. Actually, I want... |

Pei-Pei looks at all three of them, then she tenderly touches Tony and then Hsiao-Chou; then she crosses to Jin-Hua and gives her a kiss, then she leaves.

| Jin-Hua | Pei-Pei! Come back here! |

Jin-Hua is upset and goes into the shop to sit down. Hsiao-Chou follows her and sits next to her. Tony makes a move to leave, but seeing Hsiao-Chou with Jin-Hua, also goes in the shop and sits down. The lights dim down. The salesclerks bring in three tall glasses of fancy drinks. Each character reacts differently to the drinks as the lights fade out.

Act II, Scene 4
When Will the Lotus Flower Bloom?

The lights come up on the upper level of the set that now represents Grandma Jun-Mei's bedroom. Bin-Bin is sitting on the floor, Jun-Mei is in a comfortable chair. Both are reading. Transition music fades out under the dialogue.

Bin-Bin	Grandmother, where else do you still want to travel to in this world?
Jun-Mei	I don't know where else I would like to go. Let me think...the Nile River in Egypt, the Everwhite Mountain in China.
Bin-Bin	Really! What do you want to go there for?
Jun-Mei	I've been to America, Canada, Hawaii. I also went on the 21-day trip to Europe and to Bali. Remember? I went with Auntie Haluko on the Farmers' Association trip. That was very nice too.
Bin-Bin	There are the pyramids in Egypt.
Jun-Mei	Very ancient—very mystical. I also want to look at those very old forests. It seems to me that Egypt isn't

	that far away from Africa. Is that right?
Bin-Bin	Yes, Egypt is in North Africa. Well, grandmother, you're not afraid at all?
Jun-Mei	Why should I be afraid of traveling? I just want to look at those places that are so different from Taiwan. Why do you ask me about this? How about you?
Bin-Bin	I want to go places with very few people. I don't know—maybe the moon! Grandmother, how about Japan? Why don't you want to go to Japan?
Jun-Mei	Right! I have not been to Japan. Strange, I don't know why I haven't been there yet. Japan is so close to Taiwan. I think when I go, maybe I can still use my Japanese. I used to think about going to Japan a lot. When I was young, when I heard of the people coming back from Japan, my heart went thrum-thrum-thrum. Maybe I was very envious. So now if I can't go, it's okay. But if I go just to take a look, it doesn't matter.
Bin-Bin	I thought, Grandmother, that you wanted to go to Japan. Because I also want to go to Japan.
Jun-Mei	You, Bin-Bin? You just said you wanted to go to the moon! If you want to go there, you'd better start sav-

ing money now so you can buy a space ticket. Or you can become an astronaut. Then you'd better work on doing exercises and strengthening your body. Have you been studying hard lately? Read something? Or are you just reading fiction, playing electronic games? I remember you promised you wouldn't play any of those games until you go to junior high school.

Bin-Bin   I worry so much that everything I've read will be forgotten. Do you know our brain cells reduce in number every day? Every day! One hundred thousand, two hundred thousand a day!

Jun-Mei   You are afraid of forgetting and you are so young! Then how about all us grandmothers? We're not afraid of forgetting anything. Every day we read the newspapers, we read books. We just keep reading and reading. What's there to be afraid of forgetting? *(Pause)* Hey, Bin-Bin! You say that everyday we lose one hundred or two hundred thousand brain cells? Is that so? No wonder people say you get empty-headed. All the brain cells drain out!

Bin-Bin   *(Jumping up)* Sister is downstairs! Sister!

Pei-Pei doesn't answer so Bin-Bin chants a favorite children's verse.

Bin-Bin	Lotus Flower! Lotus Flower! When will you bloom?
Pei-Pei	*(Smiling, she calls back her answer.)* Not in January, maybe February.
Bin-Bin	Lotus Flower! Lotus Flower! When will you bloom?
Pei-Pei	Not in February, maybe March.

Pei-Pei slowly walks around the trees on the lower level of the set.

Bin-Bin	*(Happy, she calls to her sister.)* Pei-Pei! Sister!
Pei-Pei	*(Walking towards and behind the stairs to the upper level.)* Lotus Flower! Lotus Flower! When will you bloom? Not in March, maybe in April.
Bin-Bin	*(At the top of the stairs)* Lotus Flower! Lotus Flower! When will you bloom?
Pei-Pei	*(Climbing up the stairs)* Not in April, not in May. Not in June, not in July. Lotus Flower! Lotus Flower! When will you bloom?
Bin-Bin	In August? In September? In November? In December?
Pei-Pei	I was thinking about January of next year.

Bin-Bin	If it's in January then the newlyweds will have a warm New Year! Oh, good!
Pei-Pei	*(Sighing, she sits down next to Jun-Mei)* Grandmother! I blew it!
Jun-Mei	How come, what do you mean, you blew it? How can Lotus Flower blow it?
Pei-Pei	If you worry about what you want and what your mother wants is different than you...then you put it off.
Jun-Mei	It's all right if the Lotus Flower blooms very slowly.
Pei-Pei	This time the postponement will be very long. Grandmother, Bin-Bin...can I tell you the truth?
Jun-Mei	Which one do you want to be your husband?
Bin-Bin	I think you love them both.
Pei-Pei	I think it's impossible for a woman to love only one man throughout her life. To marry one husband is not enough. I want to marry two!
Bin-Bin	*(Giggling behind Pei-Pei)* Lotus Flower! Lotus Flower! When will you bloom? Lotus Flower! Lotus Flower! When will you bloom?
Jun-Mei	Pei-Pei, this kind of thinking...it really is too...how shall I put it? It's really too "far out"!

Bin-Bin	Why don't you just tell Mommy the truth? Mommy probably agrees with you, deep down in her heart. I always think, why has mother never had any affairs? Mommy is so romantic, so energetic, she's so pretty! As if she's in love with someone everyday. Or you can talk to Daddy. Daddy is more willing to disregard his authority. I think he will be more understanding because if there are two husbands in the house, he wouldn't have to work so much.
Jun-Mei	Pei-Pei, just speak your mind. It's better.
Pei-Pei	But mother's so mad! She was so angry in the bridal salon. What can I do?
Jun-Mei	You just walk straight down and into the shop and tell them what you just told us. But in a nicer way.
Pei-Pei	You mean I can walk straight down from here? *(She steps to the top of the stairs. Although Jun-Mei's room and the salon are in two different places, Pei-Pei understands Jun-Mei's direction to go directly from one reality to the next.)*
Bin-Bin	Yes, it's faster.
Jun-Mei	Right!
Bin-Bin	Wow! Cool! I'm going to tell my classmates and my

friends Rei-Chi and Shih-Wen! *(She runs out.)*

Jun-Mei   Me? Okay. I think I'm going to take my time to think about it. Then I'm going to tell my "classmates."

Act II, Scene 5
Two Grooms

Pei-Pei walks downstairs into the shop.

Pei-Pei Mom? *(All turn and look at her.)* I would like to explain exactly what my marriage plans are. *(She walks to Hsiao-Chou and caresses him.)* I've known you since college and in the past three or four years you have always made me so happy. And you've taught me many things. You make me feel I have someone to depend upon—I have a direction in my life. My friends at school all envy me. And you are also so handsome! I really like to be with you because you never let me feel that I'm alone.

Hsiao-Chou Love you, Pei-Pei.

Pei-Pei *(She walks to Tony and holds his hand, dancing around his chair.)* Then you walked into my life. You made me feel another kind of wild happiness. With you I can see the color and depth of the ocean. I've known you only seven months but I already feel that we have a life together. I love you. *(Hsiao-Chou responds and she speaks to him.)* And I love you too!

Jin-Hua   *(Astonished, she crosses downstage.)* I never thought my daughter would say something like this!

Pei-Pei   Both of you have proposed marriage to me. Now let me ask for your hands. If I have to be without one of you, my life is not complete. So...will you both be my grooms, please? I ask you to be my groom and his double.

No one answers and Pei-Pei turns to Jin-Hua.

Pei-Pei   Ma, I also thought that I wanted to be just like you, but I can't. To be like you is just too much. I don't think anyone can be like you. Tony, you don't have to learn from Hsiao-Chou and Hsiao-Chou, you don't have to be like Tony. In my mind I want to feel secure and I want to be wild. I wish for tenderness and I enjoy rebellion. And if I can be with both of you together, there'll be no regrets in my life. *(Both men slightly turn away.)* We were like this before—the three of us. Now, can't we just try to get along together and be married?

Sales 6	A wedding for one bride and two grooms!
Tony	Pei-Pei! Your tricks outdo my surprises!
Hsiao-Chou	Pei-Pei! I really have spoiled you rotten.
Jin-Hua	Have two husbands at the same time? What do you mean? Do you want two husbands for yourself or to marry into two households? I really can't believe my ears!
Pei-Pei	*(Nodding "yes.")* Can I? Will you?
Tony & Hsiao-Chou	No, no, Pei-Pei. No, no, no, Pei-Pei!
Sales 4	But we think the idea is really wonderful. Our bridal salon can match all your requests.
Hsiao-Chou	Well, this kind of wedding is out of the question!
Tony	Even living together like this—I myself can't take it.
Hsiao-Chou	*(To Tony)* I don't want to live with anybody like you!

Tony and Hsiao-Chou almost start to fight. Sales 6 interrupts them.

Sales 6	Don't argue! Don't fight! I think we can decide about the wedding later. But let's have a photo of one princess and her two princes together.

Sales 4	See how you feel after you see the pictures!

Tony and Hsiao-Chou sigh heavily.

Sales 6	About the suits—would you like to try on the same style silver tuxedo with blue trim?
Tony & Hsiao-Chou	Crazy!
Hsiao-Chou	I cannot accept anything like this.
Tony	Pei-Pei, your idea is really too clever. If you want me to do this, I confess right now: I can't.
Hsiao-Chou	Do you know this is more embarrassing, this is worse than if you just said you didn't love me.
Pei-Pei	Mother, you heard him. Now Hsiao-Chou doesn't want to marry me. It's not that I don't want to marry him. And right now even Tony—who you don't even want to lay your eyes on—he doesn't want me either.
Jin-Hua	Pei-Pei, I want to talk to you. I want to have a discussion with you privately. *(She tries to lead Pei-Pei to one side but Pei-Pei refuses to budge.)*
Pei-Pei	I want to have a good discussion with the two of them.

Pei-Pei tries to pull Tony and Hsiao-Chou aside with her. They hold back, but finally go along with her.

Hsiao-Chou Pei-Pei. You arc going to try to persuade me into something. But two husbands! It's really impossible!

As Pei-Pei talks sweetly to Hsiao-Chou, pulling him aside, Tony speaks to the staff.

Tony In the 21st century human beings will experience huge changes. Maybe we will become more humble! Ha ha! So, spend some time and apply your strategies. Try to persuade us. Maybe someday we'll say yes.

Tony tries to catch up with Pei-Pei and Hsiao-Chou but is stopped with a look from Jin-Hua.

Tony *(Clearing his throat)*. Ahem. Madame.

He gives her a nod of embarrassed respect, then follows Pei-Pei and Hsiao-Chou across the stage and out of the shop up left.

Act II, Scene 6
An Ideal Father

At the same time, Jin-Hua's husband enters down left and crosses to the reception area of the shop. He has seen the trio moving away. He crosses to Jin-Hua and they meet in the reception area.

Husband	Is everything all right? Where are they going? Am I late? It was difficult to park. Are you waiting for me to pay the bill?
Jin-Hua	*(Gives a little sigh.)* No. Our daughter's wedding is probably not going to happen.
Husband	Didn't they just walk away together? What happened?
Jin-Hua	Pei-Pei said in front of Hsiao-Chou...
Husband	She wants to marry Tony! Was that Tony?
Jin-Hua	Ah, it's worse than that! She said she wants to be with Tony and with Hsiao-Chou!
Husband	Is that right? What did they say about that?
Jin-Hua	What did they say? Of course they don't want that.
Husband	So our daughter is really growing up.
Jin-Hua	I never thought she would grow that "up!"

Husband	*(To the salesclerks.)* What's the charge for all the photos? Will you show me the bill? *(To Jin-Hua)* Let's go home first.
A-Hao	*(Taking out his notebook)* All the photographs they planned to shoot are not yet completed. But the formal wedding gown is already designed and the imported fabric has come in. Also, there's a small penalty clause in this contract, so the best thing to do is to go ahead and complete the photos.
Jin-Hua	What's there to shoot if there's to be no wedding?
Sales 6	There's so much to shoot, even if there's no wedding! There's the package of "Moonlight and Roses," the package of "Oath by the Mountain and by the Sea." These are not necessarily part of the wedding. Also, we have the Valentine's Dinner Special, we have the Family Reunion, the Birthday Celebration, and all kinds of packages for anniversaries! Oh, yes! How about the anniversary series for the two of you?
Jin-Hua	*(Looking at her husband)* He would never do anything like that.
Husband	"Old husband, old wife." What do we need pictures for?

| Jin-Hua | I knew that's what you were going to say. Of course, I'm an "old wife." |

The sales staff closes in, adlibbing compliments: "Very young!" "May I say you are near forty?" "You look like a sister of Miss Pei-Pei!" We've never seen any mother-in-law as young as you. "Do you not agree with us, Mr...?"

| Husband | *(He stretches his arms to move them back.)* Would you please let me and my wife have our own discussion? Okay? Really! Please. |

Reluctantly they back off and eventually exit. The husband turns to Jin-Hua.

| Husband | You are old? Then how about me? I'm even older! I can't see well. And my teeth are falling out. And my belly is getting bigger... |

Jin-Hua laughs and begins to tear up.

| Husband | You really are in tears because of Pei-Pei? Pei-Pei |

	said something that astonished you? Pei-Pei always likes to shock us, otherwise she won't say anything at all. Actually she takes after you. Both our daughters learned to speak like you.
Jin-Hua	I speak, but not like this! They don't care about other people's feelings. Besides, my words mean something. Whenever I speak I mean something.
Husband	Well, this time Pei-Pei really meant something. Does she really think that way? One woman, two men?
Jin-Hua	I don't know. I only know she and Hsiao-Chou were getting along fine and she was fooling around with Tony. If she just had two boyfriends it would be okay. But this kind of thing? *(She gestures to the dresses in the shop.)*
Husband	As a matter of fact, many women have two men. Also there are many men who have two women...
Jin-Hua	So what's that supposed to mean?
Husband	Is it happier to have love with two or to have the love of only one? This is uncertain. As for me, I feel maybe there is more happiness to have two but it is definitely more fortunate just to love one. You have to pursue happiness and it costs you a lot. But to have

the love of one is a blessing from heaven. *(She puts her head on his shoulder.)* So, my old lady—you are the blessing from heaven.

To pursue happiness, not only do you have to pay a lot, but you also have a headache all the time! Pei-Pei is a smart girl. She's not afraid of headaches. And that Tony seems fearless. Ha ha. He is a headache himself for many people. For you—whenever you think about him, your head aches!

Hsiao-Chou's personality is sort of like mine. He's very stable. He can handle almost anything. I don't think there's a problem. The affair is among the young people. Let them work it out. We shouldn't meddle in their affair.

Jin-Hua	We can't even if we wanted to.
Husband	*(Comforting her)* Our daughters, in comparison to others—of course, it's not necessary to compare—but I think they are really good, better than others. They don't have any serious problems. They never feel anxious. They aren't cold-hearted. They are always involved in something. They are very positive, self-confident and trusting. Both Pei-Pei and Bin-Bin are

	like that. I have nothing to criticize. I couldn't ask for more. And they will grow up. *(Sweetly.)* You made more effort than I.
Jin-Hua	You've talked more today than you usually do in a week!
Husband	I even used up all the talk for next month! *(Jin-Hua laughs.)* Well, you feel better now?
Jin-Hua	Ah! I was angry with Pei-Pei because she treated me like an old mother that she can never communicate with. Okay. I'll do what you say. I won't worry too much about it. Maybe I feel this way because I felt disappointed. I was going to play the flamboyant mother-in-law's role in my daughter's marriage. I got excited about it. When you and I got married we were so lonely. No family near us. Only our friends could attend the wedding at the church and come to the reception on the lawn. And the pictures! Your room-mate took them. And almost every single one is tilted! And he even got me cut out of the shot!

As Jin-Hua mentions pictures, the salesclerks appear and silently move closer, listening.

Husband	Oh, taking the pictures. Let me ask you. If you could do it again...right now...I'm not talking about taking pictures, I'm talking about getting married. The whole business—I mean that thing itself. You—the "you" now is so different. Do you think you would still marry me? I'm so down to earth, just plain folks. Not good with words, not good looking.
Jin-Hua	You were even more plain then—really a country boy. Now, as you've gotten older, you look more distinguished. But you are even more stupid! You really don't know that I am always in love with you?
Husband	Always be my bride! I know. I asked you on purpose.
Jin-Hua	And when you get old, you are even more terrible!
Husband	*(To the staff.)* Okay! We've decided to take a picture of our own.

The salesclerks rush forward and grab him. He tries to stop them.

Husband	Now let's get one thing straight. I won't wear anything weird!

The salesclerks adlib "Of course!" "Not at all."

Husband   Nothing bizarre! Just a very standard photograph.

They grab him again, reassuring him: *"Of course, of course." "Very nor-*
mal." They drag him offstage to change.

Sales 6   *(Talking with Jin-Hua, walking her upstage.)* We can
                 erase all your wrinkles!
Husband   *(Offstage)* No, no, no!

The lights in the shop fade out. Mellow music is heard.

Act II, Scene 7
Three's Still Company

A flashing gobo of light picks up Bin-Bin standing stage left. Rei-Chi joins her. They look at each other.

Bin-Bin   I like your eyes.

Rei-Chi   I like your eyebrows.

Shih-Wen appears upstage of them.

Shih-Wen   *(To Bin-Bin)* I like your lips.

Bin-Bin   *(Crossing to Shih-Wen)* I like your smile.

Shih-Wen puts his arm around her shoulder.

Shih-Wen   I like your shoulder.

Rei-Chi crosses around them, putting her arms around Bin-Bin's waist.

Rei-Chi   I like your waist.

Shih-Wen	*(Taking Bin-Bin's hand)* I like your hand.
Rei-Chi	*(Taking Bin-Bin's hand)* I like your right hand.
Bin-Bin	*(To Rei-Chi)* I also like your hand.
Bin-Bin	*(To Shih-Wen)* I like your left hand.

The three of them move downstage, taking special steps in a kind of group dance. All grow serious.

Bin-Bin	So! We really can engineer the genes to what we like the most. We can clone a better and prettier and...
Rei-Chi	Better in mathematics!
Shih-Wen	Better in examinations! Faster on the computer!
Rei-Chi	Can tell better jokes! Can act better onstage.
Bin-Bin	...self. We can clone a better self.

All three exclaim "hah!" as if to say "we can do it!"

Bin-Bin	No, no, no. We want to have a combined embryo, not a clone. Look, here is the Petrie dish for my eggs and there's the dish for your eggs.
Shih-Wen	*(Pointing to the imaginary dishes)* Bin-Bin's. Rei-Chi's.
Rei-Chi	And then we take Shih-Wen's sperm, and put them in

	Bin-Bin's dish and Rei-Chi's dish. Let them fertilize the eggs, and after a few days we can pick the embryos from the two dishes.
Shih-Wen	Pick the fat ones! Lovely ones!
Bin-Bin	They are all lovely. Make the embryos from the two dishes join together and leave them for a few hours.
Rei-Chi	That's the new embryo of Bin-Bin, Rei-Chi, and Shih-Wen.
Shih-Wen	So it's a life of a joined body.

The girls are sitting on the floor. Rei-Chi punches Shih-Wen's leg, joking.

Rei-Chi	Shih-Wen! You said you wanted to get pregnant!
Shih-Wen	Oh, I know! Last September there was the first baby conceived by three parents.
Bin-Bin	But that's not the plan I described. It's not the same as ours.
Shih-Wen	Right! What I mean is that since there's Dolly, the cloned lamb, and the three-parent baby, according to your mother's book what we are planning right now can be realized by the year 2010.
Rei-Chi	No, it must be sooner than that.

Shih-Wen	Right. And the problem of pregnancy will also be solved. I get pregnant or another kind of surrogate can carry the baby.
Rei-Chi	Yeah, just like in "Jurassic Park"!
Bin-Bin	No. *(She whispers)* The dinosaurs are hatched from eggs.

The trio has been moving towards the salon and they now reach the shop.

Bin-Bin	Ma! Ma!

Bin-Bin jumps into the shop. The lights come up suddenly. We see Jin-Hua and her husband are dressed in formal, contemporary wedding clothes. The clerks attend them.

Andy	Oh, is this your other daughter? Hello, little girl, would you like to have a picture taken together?
Bin-Bin	*(Ignoring him)* Ma! How are you? *(She sits between Jin-Hua and the Husband and says to Andy)* I don't want to have any pictures.
Jin-Hua	Bin-Bin, you always know what to say.
Husband	Did your sister tell you all about it?

Bin-Bin	*(Nodding yes)* Dad, I only want one husband. *(Both parents smile.)* But I also want a wife. *(The parents stare at each other in astonishment.)* I like girls. I also like boys. Boys and girls are different and I feel we should all be together. Then our life can be more interesting.
Husband	To like someone is different than to love someone.
Bin-Bin	Then my feeling is love.
Shih-Wen & Bin-Bin	Five-two-zero. I love you!
Rei-Chi	Five-one-two-zero. I also love you.
Bin-Bin	Five-two-zero-zero. I love you you!
All three	Seven-seven-nine-nine. Long long forever forever!
Jin-Hua	*(Angry)* Bin-Bin! Can we take a picture first?
Bin-Bin	*(She jumps down and joins Shih-Wen and Rei-Chi.)* We will get married in 2010 and then we will have a baby that belongs to the three of us. After we take the entrance exam for high school, we will search for a good hospital which has the capability to handle this genetic engineering. We will put our name on the list to reserve our place. We have been talking about this for a long time.

Husband	Jin-Hua, our little Bin-Bin is a real brain!
Andy	You will get married in 2010? If we get your parents' consent, would you like to fill out the order form right now? We're going to design a very special gown for you.
Sales 1	*(Taking out her calculator.)* Oh, let me figure it for you. Wow! By the time you have the wedding you stand to save a lot of money!

Jin-Hua, angry with the staff, rises.

Bin-Bin	Don't get nervous, Ma! I will never come to a bridal salon!

Rei-Chi, Bin-Bin and Shih-Wen all pull out their own cameras.

Rei-Chi	We can take our own pictures!

The teens begin shooting pictures of the parents and staff. The staff is a little uncomfortable with this.

Shih-Wen	We use digital cameras to take down all our memo-

	rable events and every year we make our own VCD.
Bin-Bin	We'll never need anything you do in the bridal salon. *(She joins arms with Shih-Wen and Rei-Chi.)* We know this world is not absolutely good. We also know there's parting and aging.
Shih-Wen	But by the year 2010 biochemical science will solve the problem of aging.
Rei-Chi	Yes, but there's nothing for us to worry about. It's still too early for us.
Bin-Bin	And we love. We have only one chance in our lifetime to love. So please, all the brides of the generations... *(As if uttering a prayer)*
Shih-Wen	How about the grooms?
Bin-Bin	Okay, let's say the grooms and the brides. No, the brides and the grooms. Please listen to our prayer. Please grant us a long, long summer.

The three teens begin to sing.

Bin-Bin	Grant us a perfect memory.
Shih-Wen	Grant me a tender heart.
Rei-Chi	Grant me the purest passion.

Act II

311

| Bin-Bin | I can only come to the world once, so please grant me one...*(She looks at Rei-Chi and Shih-Wen who hum the song)*...oh, please grant me more than one beautiful name so they can call me in the night, so they can grow with me and run with me in our time. We will remember forever our stories of love together. |

Their "prayer" ends softly. Then suddenly they jump into the action.

| Bin-Bin | One-two-three! And push the button! |

They position the cameras to take a shot of themselves. The flashes go off.

| Bin-Bin | Yeah! |

Just as suddenly, the teens jump up and run offstage.

| Sales 1 | Now we can take our pictures. |
| Andy | A-Hao, get the music ready. |

We hear the strains of "The Wedding" and pictures—beautiful shots—are taken.

Jeff	Now, just relax to the music. *(More pictures are taken.)*
Andy	All right, on the next one the lady should lie down and the master can sit still.

Jin-Hua, misunderstanding, lies down on the floor. The salesclerks are at first preoccupied and don't notice her. Then Andy sees her.

Andy	Oh, I'm sorry! What I mean is the master is sitting in the chair and the lady lies across his lap!
Sales 1	Oh, sorry! Such a mistake!

Jin-Hua takes the position.

Jeff	Very good! Take the shot. *(Photo is made.)*
Andy	For the next one, lady, would you please stand on the chair and hold out your leg like a flying swallow?

Andy demonstrates an arabesque. Jin-Hua assumes the position and Andy raises her lifted leg a bit. Then he gives her a fan. The husband kneels, leaning back, but he winces as his back goes out.

Andy	Please hold your fan up. Hold it up. Try to look as

relaxed as possible!

They struggle, trying to get the position right. Finally the shot is taken. The salesclerks prepare lights and set up for the next shot. Jin-Hua's veil falls. A-Hao takes it and puts it on the head of the husband.

Andy   Oh, this is not bad either! Master! Why don't you play
      your bride for your lady? And lady, why don't you
      play the groom for your master?

Sales 1   Maybe add some more lip color for him?

The salesclerks touch up the husband's make-up. They ask him to pout and smile and ad lib "try to be as sweet as your lady" etc. They position them, getting Jin-Hua to widen her stance. Finally, the awkward picture is taken.

Andy   Are you all satisfied with all this?

Jin-Hua gives a rueful nod.

Husband Satisfied? Yes, satisfied!

Andy   Would you like to try some other costumes?

Jin-Hua	I think these are good enough for us. No more!
Husband	Can we change back into our own clothes?
Sales 3	Of course you can. Please come this way.

Act II, Scene 8
You Gotta Have a Gimmick

As Jin-Hua and her husband exit, Andy and the sales staff slowly drift on stage sorting out the props and clothing pieces.

Andy   Actually, this new idea from this "young young" lady is very very interesting.

A-HAO   You mean they make all their own pictures into a VCD? The way I see them whipping out their cameras—maybe in the future they will go into our line of work.

Andy   Do you think so? You really think there are so many people who want to be in the bridal photography business?

Sales 3   Of course I think so. Even those couples who are already married for a long time would like to come back for their pictures. See, today we had that mother-bride and tomorrow we might have a grandmother-bride.

Sales 1   And I guarantee you that after a few years these ladies will come back to have another exquisite picture

	taken again to keep their beauty—to hold onto the last shreds of their youthful charm.
Sales 6	Also, there are people who get married and divorced and then married again. The bridal salon business is really hot. In Taipei every hour some couple decides to get married and every two hours someone suggests getting a divorce. So, we don't have to worry about being in the "unemployment" line.
Sales 2	Right. They just opened a new shop across the street.
Andy	They push the package of three days and two nights Singapore Honeymoon Photo Session for 6900 NT.
Sales 1	Next door they throw in 24 boxes of engagement cakes as a bonus.
Sales 3	The shop at the corner even has an offer for small families—they give household appliances—the whole set of small appliances.
Sales 4	And at the old shop up the block they put out new advertisements for a drawing to win a new car. They hang a huge red banner from the third floor to the ground to advertise it.
Sales 6	A drawing for a new car? There are drawings for diamond rings.

Sales 1	So what? In other businesses they also offer drawings for new cars—like the laundry detergent and dish soap that has that kind of contest. Even buying blue jeans has this. So what?
Andy	I agree with you. Those who want to get married— they are still looking for the professional quality of our photography. Let's not get our heads spinning about all this.
Sales 2	*(Salutes him.)* Yes sir! Each shop has its own kind of gimmicks. Maybe we should think about new slogans for ours.

He steps forward and everyone sits down to listen.

Sales 2	"As long as brides never die Our photos never cease!"

The clerks ad lib: "Oh!" "Don't say 'die'!" "How can you say that?" "Are you new here?"

Sales 2	Oh, you can't say "die" ? Let me think: "As long as brides never decrease

Bridal veils will not stop all year."

The clerks ad lib: "Too long." "That's not good." "Too many words."

Sales 2   "As long as brides never decrease

                 Bridal shops will never close."

The clerks ad lib: "Oh! You birdbrain" "Don't say 'close'!" "Never use
that word!"

Sales 2   Okay, okay.

                 "If the bride is ageless

                 The bridal shop is shameless!"

The clerks are speechless. Sales 6 finally stands up and punches Sales 2 in
the head.

Sales 6   You are shameless!

Disappointed, the staff goes back to work.

Sales 2   Oh, this is no good. This one is even worse than the others.

Andy	How can you think about something like this?
Sales 2	You're right. I have a brain deficiency.

The sales staff attends to work. Two young men enter down left, walking towards the shop. Andy gestures them in. Salesclerks greet them and bring them in, all acting most professionally. The two men exchange glances, then go into the back to change. Andy steps down to talk to the audience.

Andy   New slogans? New gimmicks? Of course, they're important. But just like this kind of couple—we started this line of photography and other shops have learned from us. Still, there aren't many photographers who can really understand their special feelings, their taste, and the poses or shots that work best for them. There are so few hairdressers who have the right sense for them. *(He smiles broadly.)* So! If I only did jobs for this kind of Prince and his Prince, I would have business aplenty!

Andy walks upstage and Jin-Hua and her husband re-enter, now in their street clothes.

Act II, Scene 9
Ageless Bride Hsio-Jen

As Jin-Hua and her husband exit, some otherworldly music drifts in and a voice upstairs is heard, reading the bridal shop advertisements.

Hsio-Jen   "21st Century Taipei Tiptop Bridal Shop. Photographs. Wedding gowns."

Sales 2   *(Alone in the shop, responding to the voice)* Here!

Hsio-Jen   You were saying "if the bride never dies..."

Sales 2   *(Seeing Hsio-Jen at the top of the stairs)* Oh, and you heard us?

Hsio-Jen   *(Walking down the stairs into the shop.)* ...and "if the bride is ageless." What else did you say?

Sales 2   Oh, I'm so sorry. We were just thinking about new slogans and I can't write them very well. *(Noticing her traditional style clothing.)* Where do you come from?

Hsio-Jen   New slogans? You can really do anything, right? This is a bridal shop?

Andy   *(Entering)* Yes and we can provide anything and everything related to a wedding. It's our profession.

Whoever wants to get married in Taipei, he or she must come to Chungshan North Road. And if you are wise enough to visit our one-hundred-year-old shop, you are just like a fish jumping into the water!

Hsio-Jen   A one-hundred-year-old shop. *(She laughs, moving her hands in a gesture that suggests a fish swimming; she turns, dancing.)* Fish in the river! *(She becomes serious.)* So you can re-do a wedding of mine? Can you? Let me, this *(she whispers the word)* ageless, never-die bride have her wish come true?

Andy   *(Raising his voice to the staff offstage)* An ancient-style wedding. Do you all remember?

Jeff   Of course we remember!

Sales 3   No problem!

All the salesclerks enter and immediately take their positions. Meanwhile, Jin-Hua and her husband have been slowly leaving the shop, going into the reception area, then across the downstage area to exit down right. Just before they exit, Jin-Hua stops, listening to the voice of Hsio-Jen.

Jin-Hua   That voice that was talking. It sounded like my mother when she was young. No, it almost has a tone older

than my mom's—my mother's mother! That kind of
quality.

*Looking back and seeing nothing, Jin-Hua and the husband chat as they
exit down right. Meanwhile, Sales 3 enters with an old-fashioned red veil
and crosses to Hsio-Jen to help her put it on.*

Hsio-Jen   Let me do it myself.

*Hsio-Jen looks in the mirror, puts on some make-up, and then starts to put
the veil on her head. But she places it aside and takes a modern white veil,
putting in on her head instead. She crosses to Jeff, and they move as if
walking down the aisle. She turns to him and looks at him earnestly. Then
she addresses Andy.*

Hsio-Jen   I don't want this one. May I reject him? *(To Jeff.)* I
            don't want you. Here, I'd like to return this merchan-
            dise.
Andy   That's no problem! But a quick change of partner
            causes us so much trouble...

Hsio-Jen smiles knowingly and pulls out a red envelope, offering it to Andy.

Hsio-Jen	Will this do? *(Andy takes it, nodding his approval.)*
Jeff	So who do you want to get married to?
Hsio-Jen	This is none of your business. I'll look for him myself.
Andy	Good. Choose your own groom!

At once all the male members of the sales staff strike a pose, listening as Hsio-Jen walks around, looking over her choices.

Hsio-Jen	Too tall. Too strange. Too mean. Too funny. *(To Andy)* These are all you have? *(She steps out of the shop and peers into the audience.)* Is there anybody there? *(She cannot see well and reveals that she is anxious and disappointed.)* Hundred-year-old shop...it's a very long wait. Let me be a real bride.
	(She begins to remember) His...his...he...he...he must be waiting for me under that tree. He must be there. I'm sure he will still be there! *(Her face lights up as she addresses her childhood sweetheart.)* I'm here! Hello! I'm here now. Your bride is here for you! Don't play hide-and-seek with me. Please believe me. I'm really here this time.
	(Remembering.) "1" "2" "3" "4" "5" ... "1" "2"

"3" "4" " 5." Where is my friend?

As Hsio-Jen sings the childhood song, we hear a voice in the back of the
auditorium, harmonizing with her. The sweetheart runs through the house
and jumps onstage to join Hsio-Jen at the finish of the song.

Hsio-Jen &
Sweetheart

One, two, three. Where can he be?

Five, four, three. Can she see me?

Six, seven, eight. Is he at my gate?

Two, three, four. Here he is at my door!

Andy gestures for the two of them to stand together.

Andy   First, bow to heaven and bow to the earth.

Hsio-Jen and the sweetheart face front and bow.

Andy   Second, bow to the parents.

All the sales staff rush to the antique chairs in the reception room, position-
ing themselves as the family. Hsio-Jen and the sweetheart turn upstage and

give them a formal bow.

Andy   Third, the bride and groom bow to each other and we
      will send you off to your love nest.

*Hsio-Jen faces her sweetheart and they bow. Andy pushes the sweetheart
closer to Hsio-Jen as an upbeat version of the "Wedding March" is heard.
Hsio-Jen and her sweetheart kiss. Then they walk upstage and turn back to
the front. The music segues into a popular, contemporary dance tune. The
whole sales staff dances with abandon as the other characters all enter and
join in the dance, which segues into the curtain call.*

*First, Bin-Bin, Rei-Chi, and Sheh-Wen jump onstage, hand in hand, and
dance, going upstairs and down around the stairs. Grandma Jun-Mei joins
Jin-Hua and Jin-Hua's husband up on the second level of the stage. They
dance, matching the rhythm of the others.*

*Pei-Pei appears with Hsiao-Chou and Tony. They dance in unison, moving
to centerstage. As they turn together and cross past one another, Tony and
Hsiao-Chou suddenly realize they are dancing with each other, rather than
with Pei-Pei. They retreat quickly, turning back to Pei-Pei. After a while
this action repeats and the men find themselves partners once more. Pei-*

Pei steps between them, smiling, and links arms with each one.

The tempo grows faster and the joy and energy of the dance builds to a peak as the curtain falls.

The End

From the Translator

Working on the translation of "The Bride and Her Double" has been one of the most remarkable experiences of my Fulbright year in Taiwan. Not only did I discover an absolutely charming and original theatre production, but in creating the translation. I also learned about marriage and family traditions, Chinese history, and the amazing phenomenon of the bridal photo salon. "The Bride and Her Double" was the first live, full-length contemporary play performed in Chinese that I had ever seen. The performances and the story enchanted me. As I got to know the script indepth, I was even more impressed with its social commentary, topicality and theatricality.

I have always believed that the best translations should be written by two people—one whose native language is the same as the original text and a native speaker of the second language. Ideally, it would have been helpful if I was fluent in Chinese, but Chi-Mei Wang's excellent command of English made it possible for us to derive the English text in tandem. Our process was to get together once or twice a week and go through the script. Professor Wang would read the lines in a quick, literal English translation, then together we would discuss the best way to express the thought and character in English. We aimed to make the inner meanings of the lines clear and the speech natural, fluid, and actable in English. I tried to look at the script as a director might when approaching it for the first time. So we added setting details, some pronunciation and production notes. After each meeting I would write up the rough translation and later we would review it and refine it.

The most important aspect of our process was being able to discuss a line of text or a character action and come to a mutual understangind of its meaning. We always endeavored to find the exact word or phrase that would carry the same thought and feelings in English that it did in Chinese. As the playwright and director of the Taiwan production, Professor Wang shared with me the extensive research and investigation of the bridal salons that inform the play. In the way, the translation has become more than just literal recording of the Chinese words—it is, we hope, a translation of Chinese and Taiwanese culture and society.

That is why creating the translation was such a satisfying experience for me. I believe this project has given me insight into Asian culture that I could not have attained in any other way. I gained more than information— which I might have read in a book. No, my experience was much more enriching. It is the difference in visiting a foreign place and staying in a hotel and getting around in taxis, or being a guest in the home of someone who takes you on a personal tour of the city. Through this process that which was exotic has become familiar and (although I will be the first to admit that I have so much more to learn) I believe I now have a much greater understanding and a deeper appreciation of Taiwan and its people. I don't know that I could have ever come to feel so at home in Taiwan any other way.

All along I have maintained the hope that the English script of "The Bride and Her Double" will be performed in Americal. I plan to direct a production at the earliest possible moment. But I hope many companies will perform the script. One thing I would like to say is that the script can easily be staged with or without Asian actors. "The Bride and Her Double" is no different than, for example, Brecht's Good Woman of Szechwan or the opera Turandot, both of which are set in China but are most often produced with Western performers. It is true that the backdrop of the play is about Chinese and Taiwanese wedding traditions. But its main action is about the struggle of five women in four generations to earn the right to choose a husband and to deal with a lack of freedom of choice or (in the youngest generation) a surfeit of freedom. The secondary action stems from the problems of young people trying to make a living in a service industry and to get ahead in the world. These problems are universal and will speak to audiences everywhere. So I hope American audiences will soon be able to experience the delight that the Taipei audiences derived from "The Bride and Her Double."

I would like to give special thanks to The Foundation for Scholarly Exchange (the Fulbright program in Taiwan) and to the National Endowment for Arts and Culture of Taiwan for selecting me as a Fulbright grantee. I would also like to thank my home institution, Winthrop University, for giving me sabbatical leave this year. Without their support, this project would not have been possible.

Sincerely,

Jeannie M. Woods

Jeannie M. Woods, Ph.D.
Senior Fulbright Scholar to Taiwan, 1998-99
Associate Professor of Theatre
Artistic Director of The New Stage Ensemble
Winthrop University, Rock Hill, South Carolina

國家圖書館出版品預行編目資料

複製新娘=The bride and her double／汪其楣著
　　——初版——臺北市：遠流，2000〔民89〕
　　面；　　　公分——（戲劇館）
　　劇本中英對照
　　ISBN 957-32-3909-4（平裝）

854.6　　　　　　　　　　　　　　89000544